SCIENTIFIC AMERICAN EXPLORES BIG IDEAS

Cyberattacks

I0112426

The Editors of *Scientific American*

SCIENTIFIC AMERICAN EDUCATIONAL PUBLISHING

Published in 2024 by Scientific American Educational Publishing
in association with **The Rosen Publishing Group**
2544 Clinton Street, Buffalo NY 14224

Contains material from Scientific American®, a division of Springer Nature America, Inc.,
reprinted by permission, as well as original material from The Rosen Publishing Group®.

Copyright © 2024 Scientific American® and Rosen Publishing Group®.

All rights reserved.

First Edition

Scientific American
Lisa Pallatroni: Project Editor

Rosen Publishing
David Kuchta: Compiling Editor
Michael Moy: Senior Graphic Designer

Cataloging-in-Publication Data
Names: Scientific American, Inc.
Title: Cyberattacks / edited by the Scientific American Editors.
Description: First Edition. | New York : Scientific American Educational Publishing, 2024. |
Series: Scientific American explores big ideas | Includes bibliographical references and index.
Identifiers: ISBN 9781725350151 (pbk.) | ISBN 9781725350168
(library bound) | ISBN 9781725350175 (ebook)
Subjects: LCSH: Cyberterrorism–Juvenile literature. | Extortion–
Juvenile literature. | Computer crimes–Juvenile literature.
Classification: LCC HV6773.15.C97 C938 2024 | DDC 363.325–dc23

Manufactured in the United States of America
Websites listed were live at the time of publication.

Cover: Rawpixel.com/Shutterstock.com

CPSIA Compliance Information: Batch # CWSA24.
For Further Information contact Rosen Publishing at 1-800-237-9932.

CONTENTS

Introduction   6

Section 1: The Age of Cyberwar   7

1.1   AI-Influenced Weapons Need Better Regulation   8
By Branka Marijan

1.2   Are We Ready for the Future of Warfare?   12
By Terry C. Wallace Jr.

1.3   Fully Autonomous Weapons Pose Unique Dangers to Humankind   15
By Noel Sharkey

1.4   Here's How to End the Fog of Cyber War   25
By The Editors of *Scientific American*

1.5   Here's What a Cyber Warfare Arsenal Might Look Like   27
By Larry Greenemeier

Section 2: Infrastructure Under Attack   31

2.1   Hacker Attack on Essential Pipeline Shows Infrastructure Weaknesses   32
By Sophie Bushwick

2.2   How Hackers Tried to Add Dangerous Lye into a City's Water Supply   36
By Sophie Bushwick

2.3   Is the Power Grid Getting More Vulnerable to Cyber Attacks?   39
By Jesse Dunietz

2.4   The Most Vulnerable Ransomware Targets Are the Institutions We Rely On Most   44
By Annie Sneed

2.5   U.S. Hospitals Not Immune to Crippling Cyber Attacks   48
By Dina Fine Maron

2.6   Urban Bungle: Atlanta Cyber Attack Puts Other Cities on Notice   51
By Larry Greenemeier

2.7   What Do Hurricanes and Cybersecurity Have in Common?   55
By Algirde Pipikaite, Haiyan Song

Section 3: Big Data In the Wrong Hands   59

3.1   Blockchain Enhances Privacy, Security and Conveyance
       of Data   60
       By Mihaela Ulieru

3.2   Data Thieves Find Easy Pickings in the Health Care System 63
       By Adam Tanner

3.3   Data Vu: Why Breaches Involve the Same Stories Again
       and Again   67
       By Daniel J. Solove, Woodrow Hartzog

3.4   Giant U.S. Computer Security Breach Exploited Very
       Common Software   71
       By Sophie Bushwick

3.5   The Equifax Hack—Bad for Them, Worse for Us   75
       By Paul Rosenzweig

Section 4: Are Our Elections Vulnerable?   78

4.1   Are Blockchains the Answer for Secure Elections?
       Probably Not   79
       By Jesse Dunietz

4.2   How to Defraud Democracy   84
       By J. Alex Halderman, Jen Schwartz

4.3   The Vulnerabilities of Our Voting Machines   93
       By Jen Schwartz

Section 5: White Hats vs. Black Hats   100

5.1   CSI: Cyber-Attack Scene Investigation:
       a Malware Whodunit   101
       By Larry Greenemeier

5.2   FBI Takes Down Hive Criminal Ransomware Group   105
       By Sophie Bushwick

5.3   Hacking the Ransomware Problem   110
       By The Editors of Scientific American

5.4   The Imperfect Crime: How the WannaCry Hackers
       Could Get Nabbed   113
       By Jesse Dunietz

5.5   Women in Cybersecurity: Where We Are and Where
       We're Going   117
       By Nahal Shahidzadeh

Section 6: Protecting Your Privacy   122

6.1   Congressional Ignorance Leaves the U.S. Vulnerable to
Cyberthreats   123
By Jackson Barnett

6.2   Misdiagnosing Our Cyberhealth   126
By Emily Balcetis

6.3   Passwords Are on the Way Out, and It's about Time   130
By David Pogue

6.4   Social Security Numbers Aren't Secure: What Should
We Use Instead?   133
By Sophie Bushwick

6.5   The Mathematics of (Hacking) Passwords   137
By Jean-Paul Delahaye

6.6   How Cryptojacking Can Corrupt the Internet of Things   152
By Larry Greenemeier

Glossary   156
Further Information   157
Citations   158
Index   159

INTRODUCTION

Cyberattacks are among the greatest threats to society today. All it takes is ingenuity and persistence on the part of bad actors, sloppy workmanship on the part of software developers, and gullibility on the part of Internet users, and a nuclear power plant can go haywire, a hospital's electricity can be cut off in the middle of someone's heart surgery, the credit card numbers of millions of consumers can be stolen, the emergency services of an entire city can be shut down, or war can be launched on unsuspecting nations.

The ways in which cyberattacks can wreak havoc on our interconnected society are as infinite as the connections themselves. In Section 1, we look at cyberattacks among nation states, where cyberwar replaces soldiers with hackers, bullets with electrons, but present threats are just as real. Section 2 narrows the focus to threats to the dams, oil and gas pipelines, electrical grids, hospitals, and other critical infrastructure that we rely on every day. Section 3 shifts to attacks on large corporations and financial services, where the credit card, bank account, and social security numbers of millions if not billions of individuals are kept secret. Section 4 looks briefly at the threat to the integrity of our elections. Finally, the last two chapters shift from threats to protections: Section 5 looks at the efforts being made by cybersecurity professionals (the "white hats") to protect us from malevolent attacks by the "black hats," while Section 6 focuses on what individuals can do to protect themselves in their everyday lives.

If all these topics make you nervous to ever go online again, that's a good thing. Cyberattacks happen most often when individuals let down their guard, click on a link or download pirated software or videos they shouldn't, or give away information to someone they think they can trust. We willingly hand over our data and our security to anonymous corporations and government institutions we expect to protect us, and they must do their job keeping us safe, but we have to do our job as well.

Section 1: The Age of Cyberwar

1.1   AI-Influenced Weapons Need Better Regulation
      By Branka Marijan

1.2   Are We Ready for the Future of Warfare?
      By Terry C. Wallace Jr.

1.3   Fully Autonomous Weapons Pose Unique Dangers to Humankind
      By Noel Sharkey

1.4   Here's How to End the Fog of Cyber War
      By The Editors of *Scientific American*

1.5   Here's What a Cyber Warfare Arsenal Might Look Like
      By Larry Greenemeier

AI-Influenced Weapons Need Better Regulation

By Branka Marijan

With Russia's invasion of Ukraine as the backdrop, the United Nations recently held a meeting to discuss the use of autonomous weapons systems, commonly referred to as killer robots. These are essentially weapons that are programmed to find a class of targets, then select and attack a specific person or object within that class, with little human control over the decisions that are made.

Russia took center stage in this discussion, in part because of its potential capabilities in this space, but also because its diplomats thwarted the effort to discuss these weapons, saying sanctions made it impossible to properly participate. For a discussion that to date had been far too slow, Russia's spoiling slowed it down even further.

I have been tracking the development of autonomous weapons and attending the UN discussions on the issue for over seven years, and Russia's aggression is becoming an unfortunate test case for how artificial intelligence (AI)–fueled warfare can and likely will proceed.

The technology behind some of these weapons systems is immature and error-prone, and there is little clarity on how the systems function and make decisions. Some of these weapons will invariably hit the wrong targets, and competitive pressures might result in deployment of more systems that are not ready for the battlefield.

To avoid the loss of innocent lives and the destruction of critical infrastructure in Ukraine and beyond, we need nothing less that the strongest diplomatic effort to prohibit in some cases, and regulate, in others, the use of these weapons and the technologies behind them, including AI and machine learning. This is critical because when military operations are proceeding, poorly countries might be tempted to use new technologies to gain an advantage. An example of this is Russia's KUB-BLA loitering munition, which has the ability to identify targets using AI.

Data fed into AI-based systems can teach remote weapons what a target looks like, and what to do upon reaching that target. While similar to facial recognition tools, AI technologies for military use have different implications, particularly when they are meant to destroy and kill, and as such, experts have raised concerns about their introduction into dynamic war contexts. And while Russia may have been successful in thwarting real-time discussion of these weapons, it isn't alone. The U.S., India and Israel are all fighting regulation of these dangerous systems.

AI might be more mature and well-known in its use in cyberwarfare, including to supercharge malware attacks or to better impersonate trusted users in order to access to critical infrastructure, such as the electric grid. But, major powers are using it to develop physically destructive weapons. Russia has already made important advances in autonomous tanks, machines that can run without human operators who could theoretically override mistakes, while the United States has demonstrated a number of capabilities, including munitions that can destroy a surface vessel using a swarm of drones. AI is employed in the development of swarming technologies and loitering munitions, also called kamikaze drones. Rather than the futuristic robots seen in science-fiction movies, these systems use previously existing military platforms that leverage AI technologies. Simply, a few lines of code and new sensors can make a difference in whether a military system is functioning autonomously or under human control. Crucially, introducing AI into decision-making by militaries could lead to over-reliance on the technology, shaping military decision-making and potentially escalating conflicts.

AI-based warfare might seem like a video game, but last September, according to Secretary of the Air Force Frank Kendall, the U.S. Air Force, for the first time, used AI to help to identify a target or targets in "a live operational kill chain." Presumably, this means AI was used to identify and kill human targets.

Little information was provided about the mission, including whether any casualties that occurred were the intended targets. What inputs were used to identify such individuals and could there have been possible errors in identification? AI technologies have been shown to be biased, particularly against women and people in minority communities. False identifications disproportionately impact already marginalized and racialized groups.

If recent social media discussions among the AI community are any indication, the developers, largely from the private sector, who are creating the new technologies that some militaries are already deploying are largely unaware of their impact. Tech journalist Jeremy Kahn argues in *Fortune* that a dangerous disconnect exists between developers and leading militaries, including U.S. and Russian, which are using AI in decision-making and data analysis. The developers seem to be unaware of the general-purpose nature of some of the tools they are building and how militaries could use them in warfare, including to target civilians.

Undoubtedly, lessons from the current invasion will also shape the technology projects the militaries pursue. At the moment, the United States is at the head of the pack, but a joint statement by Russia and China in early February notes that they aim to "jointly build international relations of a new type," and specifically points to their aim to shape governance of new technologies, including what I believe will be military uses of AI.

Independently, the U.S. and its allies are developing norms on responsible military uses of AI, but generally are not talking with potential adversaries. In general, states with more technologically advanced militaries have been unwilling to accept any constraints on the developments of AI technology. This is where international diplomacy is critical: there must be constraints on these types of weapons, and everyone has to agree to shared standards and transparency in use of the technologies.

The war in Ukraine should be a wake-up call regarding the use of technology in warfare, and the need to regulate AI technologies to ensure civilian protection. Unchecked and potentially hasty development of military applications of artificial intelligence will continue to undermine international humanitarian law and norms regarding civilian protection. Though the international order is in disarray, the solutions to current and future crises are diplomatic, not military, and the next gathering of the U.N. or another group needs to rapidly address this new era of warfare.

About the Author

Branka Marijan is a senior researcher at Project Ploughshares, where she leads research on the military and security implications of emerging technologies. She is a contributor to the Center for International Governance Innovation.

Are We Ready for the Future of Warfare?

By Terry C. Wallace Jr.

W arfare has always been about exerting political will. In the most basic way, that's accomplished by one side inflicting enough pain on the other to compel them to acquiesce—and technology has always played a key role in doing that. The Greek phalanx, the crossbow, the cannon, poison gas: all introduced new, powerful methods of destruction on the battlefield and fundamentally changed the way war was fought.

Today, however, science and technology are being used to exert political will far from the traditional battlefield. Adversaries are exploiting space, cyberattacks, biology and other emerging technologies to significantly disrupt the systems underpinning our society—including telecommunications infrastructure, power grids, public health systems, transportation systems and financial institutions. In short, an adversary can gain advantage without ever firing a shot.

In some ways, these "new" types of attacks are anything but. The world's first cyberattack occurred in 1834, when two French bankers hacked the government's mechanical telegraph system, allowing them to get information about the markets far in advance of their competitors. Then there was the bio attack by the Mongol army in 1346, when it catapulted plague-infected cadavers into the besieged city of Caffa (now Feodosia, Ukraine) to spread the Black Death among its enemies.

But what has changed is the scale and speed of technology. For example, for a group to have a presence in space no longer requires billions of dollars and a nation-state sponsor. Small satellites that cost only a few thousand dollars can hitch rides on rockets into low Earth orbit for a remarkably low fee. These lunchbox-sized (and smaller) satellites hold enormous potential for national security. Space has become essential infrastructure. It is the hub for everything from GPS to communications, and our reliance on it has spurred a sense of urgency to both protect our space assets and make our infrastructure more resilient. Small satellites can aid in that by bolstering the nation's GPS satellites or helping troops communicate in remote areas. But their affordability makes them easily accessible to terrorist groups and other enemy organizations as well.

Cybercrime is another threat that can wreak havoc on a grand scale in a matter of minutes. The WannaCry computer virus infected 200,000 computers across 150 countries and shut down hospitals in the United Kingdom last year. In 2008, a flash drive containing malicious computer code created by a foreign intelligence agency was uploaded to a network run by the U.S. Central Command, infecting both classified and unclassified systems and allowing for the transfer of data to foreign servers.

While weaponizing diseases has proven more difficult, the anthrax attack in 2001 that killed five people, infected 17 more and caused nationwide alarm is a reminder of the potential for a bio attack to kill and disrupt. This year, Germany arrested a man on suspicion of planning a ricin attack. As Bill Gates recently noted, even something as seemingly mundane as the flu could be weaponized, killing millions and hobbling the world's economy. In addition, our ability to manipulate genes—while promising when applied to searching for cures to previously incurable diseases—also has the potential to be weaponized. What if a nation could make its own population immune to a disease while the rest of the world is still defenseless?

Because weakness in any of these areas can leave our nation vulnerable, our continued security lies in keeping our science and technology a step ahead.

In space, we must be quick and agile to outpace our adversaries or risk losing our superiority in that domain. Developing new, small satellites is part of that strategy, but so is continuing to develop better fuels for long-term exploration, and better technologies to improve communications and optical sensors that can provide key intelligence information.

Cyberattacks can be thwarted through improved encryption and other tools. In 2016, China launched the world's first hack-proof communications satellite—using quantum encryption—and stoked fears that the U.S. is falling behind in the cybersecurity race. In fact, the U.S. has the same capability with unhackable quantum encryption tools developed at Los Alamos National Laboratory; they just haven't been deployed on the same scale as in China. Broader adoption of quantum encryption in the U.S. would enhance our security.

Protecting against biowarfare starts with understanding the movement of diseases through populations. We're using artificial intelligence to combine satellite imagery with social media posts and online searches about diseases to help predict outbreaks before they become epidemic. In the case of a bio attack, early warning could stem the disease spread and save thousands of lives. We need to stop thinking about warfare as only lines on a map, firepower and territory. Our nation's scientists and engineers are now, in many ways, on the front lines. To successfully deter our adversaries and keep our nation safe, we must maintain a scientific and technical advantage in these new arenas of combat. Our future depends on it.

About the Author

Terry C. Wallace, Jr., is the director of Los Alamos National Laboratory in New Mexico.

Fully Autonomous Weapons Pose Unique Dangers to Humankind

By Noel Sharkey

I n September 2019 a swarm of 18 bomb-laden drones and seven cruise missiles overwhelmed Saudi Arabia's advanced air defenses to crash into the Abqaiq and Khurais oil fields and their processing facilities. The surprisingly sophisticated attack, which Yemen's Houthi rebels claimed responsibility for, halved the nation's output of crude oil and natural gas and forced an increase in global oil prices. The drones were likely not fully autonomous, however: they did not communicate with one another to pick their own targets, such as specific storage tanks or refinery buildings. Instead each drone appears to have been preprogrammed with precise coordinates to which it navigated over hundreds of kilometers by means of a satellite positioning system.

Fully autonomous weapons systems (AWSs) may be operating in war theaters even as you read this article, however. Turkey has announced plans to deploy a fleet of autonomous Kargu quadcopters against Syrian forces in early 2020, and Russia is also developing aerial swarms for that region. Once launched, an AWS finds, tracks, selects and attacks targets with violent force, all without human supervision.

Autonomous weapons are not self-aware, humanoid "Terminator" robots conspiring to take over; they are computer-controlled tanks, planes, ships and submarines. Even so, they represent a radical change in the nature of warfare. Humans are outsourcing the decision to kill to a machine—with no one watching to ascertain the legitimacy of an attack before it is carried out. Since the mid-2000s, when the U.S. Department of Defense triggered a global artificial-intelligence arms race by signaling its intent to develop autonomous weapons for all branches of the armed forces, every major power and several lesser ones have been striving to acquire these systems. According to U.S. Secretary of Defense Mark Esper, China is already exporting AWSs to the Middle East.

The military attractions of autonomous weapons are manifold. For example, the U.S. Navy's X-47B, an unmanned fighter jet that can land and take off from aircraft carriers even in windy conditions and refuel in the air, will have 10 times the reach of piloted fighter jets. The U.S. has also developed an unmanned transoceanic warship called *Sea Hunter*, to be accompanied by a flotilla of DASH (Distributed Agile Submarine Hunting) submarines. In January 2019 the *Sea Hunter* traveled from San Diego to Hawaii and back, demonstrating its suitability for use in the Pacific. Russia is automating its state-of-the-art T-14 Armata tank, presumably for deployment at the European border; meanwhile weapons manufacturer Kalashnikov has demonstrated a fully automated combat module to be mounted on existing weapons systems (such as artillery guns and tanks) to enable them to sense, choose and attack targets. Not to be outdone, China is working on AI-powered tanks and warships, as well as a supersonic autonomous air-to-air combat aircraft called Anjian, or Dark Sword, that can twist and turn so sharply and quickly that the g-force generated would kill a human pilot.

Given such fierce competition, the focus is inexorably shifting to ever faster machines and autonomous drone swarms, which can overwhelm enemy defenses with a massive, multipronged and coordinated attack. Much of the push toward such weapons comes from defense contractors eyeing the possibility of large profits, but high-ranking military commanders nervous about falling behind in the artificial-intelligence arms race also play a significant role. Some nations, in particular the U.S. and Russia, are looking only at the potential military advantages of autonomous systems—a blinkered view that prevents them from considering the disturbing scenarios that can unfold when rivals catch up.

As a roboticist, I recognized the necessity of meaningful human control over weapons systems when I first learned of the plans to build AWSs. We are facing a new era in warfare, much like the dawn of the atomic age. It does not take a historian to realize that once a new class of weapon is in the arsenals of military powers, its use will incrementally expand, placing humankind at risk of conflicts that can barely be imagined today. In 2009 I and three other academics set up the International Committee for Robot Arms Control, which later teamed up with other nongovernmental organizations (NGOs) to form the Campaign to Stop Killer Robots. Now a coalition of 130 NGOs from 60 countries, the campaign seeks to persuade the United Nations to negotiate a legally binding treaty that would prohibit the development, testing and production of weapons that select targets and attack them with violent force without meaningful human control.

Time to Think

The ultimate danger of systems for warfare that take humans out of the decision-making loop is illustrated by the true story of "the man who saved the world." In 1983 Lieutenant Colonel Stanislav Petrov was on duty at a Russian nuclear early-warning center when his computer sounded a loud alarm and the word "LAUNCH" appeared in bold red letters on his screen—indications that a U.S. nuclear missile was fast approaching. Petrov held his nerve and waited. A second launch warning rang out, then a third and a fourth. With the fifth, the red "LAUNCH" on his screen changed to "MISSILE STRIKE." Time was ticking away for the U.S.S.R. to retaliate, but Petrov continued his deliberation. "Then I made my decision," Petrov said in a BBC interview in 2013. "I would not trust the computer." He reported the nuclear attack as a false alarm—even though he could not be certain. As it turned out, the onboard computing system on the Soviet satellites had misclassified sunlight reflecting off clouds as the engines of intercontinental ballistic missiles.

This tale illustrates the vital role of deliberative human decision-making in war: given those inputs, an autonomous system would have decided to fire. But making the right call takes time. A hundred years' worth of psychological research tells us that if we do not take at least a minute to think things over, we will overlook contradictory information, neglect ambiguity, suppress doubt, ignore the absence of confirmatory evidence, invent causes and intentions, and conform with expectations. Alarmingly, an oft-cited rationale for AWSs is that conflicts are unfolding too quickly for humans to be making the decisions.

"It's a lot faster than me," Bruce Jette, a U.S. Army acquisitions officer, said last October to *Defense News*, referring to a targeting system for tanks. "I can't see and think through some of the things it can calculate nearly as fast as it can." In fact, speed is a key reason that partially autonomous weapons are already in use for some defensive operations, which require that the detection of, evaluation of and response to a threat be completed within seconds. These systems—variously known as SARMO (Sense and React to Military Objects), automated and automatic weapons systems—include Israel's Iron Dome for protecting the country from rockets and missiles; the U.S. Phalanx cannon, mounted on warships to guard against attacks from antiship missiles or helicopters; and the German NBS Mantis gun, used to shoot down smaller munitions such as mortar shells. They are localized, are defensive, do not target humans and are switched on by humans in an emergency—which is why they are not considered fully autonomous.

The distinction is admittedly fine, and weapons on the cusp of SARMO and AWS technology are already in use. Israel's Harpy and Harop aerial drones, for instance, are explosive-laden rockets launched prior to an air attack to clear the area of antiaircraft installations. They cruise around hunting for radar signals, determine whether the signals come from friend or foe and, if the latter, dive-bomb on the assumption that the radar is connected to an antiaircraft installation. In May 2019 secretive Israeli drones—according to one report, Harops—blew up Russian-made air-defense systems in Syria.

These drones are "loitering munitions" and speed up only when attacking, but several fully autonomous systems will range in speed from fast subsonic to supersonic to hypersonic. For example, the U.S.'s Defense Advanced Research Projects Agency (DARPA) has tested the Falcon unmanned hypersonic aircraft at speeds around 20 times the speed of sound—approximately 21,000 kilometers per hour.

In addition to speed, militaries are pursuing "force multiplication"—increases in the destructive capacity of a weapons system—by means of autonomous drones that cooperate like wolves in a pack, communicating with one another to choose and hunt individual targets. A single human can launch a swarm of hundreds (or even thousands) of armed drones into the air, on the land or water, or under the sea. Once the AWS has been deployed, the operator becomes at best an observer who could abort the attack—if communication links have not been broken.

To this end, the U.S. is developing swarms of fixed-wing drones such as Perdix and Gremlin, which can travel long distances with missiles. DARPA has field-tested the coordination of swarms of aerial quadcopters (known for their high maneuverability) with ground vehicles, and the Office of Naval Research has demonstrated a fleet of 13 boats that can "overwhelm an adversary." The China Electronics Technology Group, in a move that reveals the country's intentions, has (separately) tested a group of 200 fixed-wing drones, as well as 56 small drone ships for attacking enemy warships. In contrast, Russia seems to be mainly interested in tank swarms that can be used for coordinated attacks or be laid out to defend national borders.

Gaming the Enemy

The Petrov story also shows that although computers may be fast, they are often wrong. Even now, with the incredible power and speed of modern computing and sensor processing, AI systems can err in many unpredictable ways. In 2012 the Department of Defense acknowledged the potential for such computer issues with autonomous weapons and asserted the need to minimize human errors, failures in human-machine interactions, malfunctions, degradation of communications and coding glitches in software. Apart from these self-evident safeguards, autonomous systems would also have to be protected from subversion by adversaries via cyberattacks, infiltration of the industrial supply chain, jamming of signals, spoofing (misleading of positioning systems) and deployment of decoys.

In reality, protecting against disruptions by the enemy will be extremely difficult, and the consequences of these assaults could be dire. Jamming would block communications so that an operator would not be able to abort attacks or redirect weapons. It could disrupt coordination between robotic weapons in a swarm and make them run out of control. Spoofing, which sends a strong false GPS signal, can cause devices to lose their way or be guided to crash into buildings.

Decoys are real or virtual entities that deceive sensors and targeting systems. Even the most sophisticated artificial-intelligence systems can easily be gamed. Researchers have found that a few dots or lines cleverly added to a sign, in such a way as to be unnoticeable to humans, can mislead a self-driving car so that it swerves into another lane against oncoming traffic or ignores a stop sign. Imagine the kinds of problems such tricks could create for autonomous weapons. Onboard computer controllers could, for example, be fooled into mistaking a hot dog stand for a tank.

Most baffling, however, is the last directive on the Defense Department's list: minimizing "other enemy countermeasures or actions, or unanticipated situations on the battlefield." It is impossible to minimize unanticipated situations on the battlefield because you cannot minimize what you cannot anticipate. A conflict zone will feature a potentially infinite number of unforeseeable circumstances; the very essence of conflict is to surprise the enemy. When it comes to AWSs, there are many ways to trick sensor processing or disrupt computer-controlled machinery.

One overwhelming computer problem the Department of Defense's directive misses, rather astonishingly, is the unpredictability of machine-machine interactions. What happens when enemy autonomous weapons confront one another? The worrisome answer is that no one knows or can know. Every AWS will have to be controlled by a top-secret computer algorithm. Its combat strategy will have to be unknown to others to prevent successful enemy countermeasures. The secrecy makes sense from a security perspective—but it dramatically reduces the predictability of the weapons' behavior.

A clear example of algorithmic confrontation run amok was provided by two booksellers, bordeebook and profnath, on the Amazon Web site in April 2011. Usually the out-of-print 1992 book *The Making of a Fly* sold for around $50 plus $3.99 shipping. But every time bordeebook increased its price, so did profnath; that, in turn, increased bordeebook's price, and so on. Within a week bordeebook was selling the book for $23,698,655.93 plus $3.99 shipping before anyone noticed. Two simple and highly predictable computer algorithms went out of control because their clashing strategies were unknown to competing sellers.

Although this mispricing was harmless, imagine what could happen if the complex combat algorithms of two swarms of autonomous weapons interacted at high speed. Apart from the uncertainties introduced by gaming with adversarial images, jamming, spoofing, decoys and cyberattacks, one must contend with the impossibility of predicting the outcome when computer algorithms battle it out. It should be clear that these weapons represent a very dangerous alteration in the nature of warfare. Accidental conflicts could break out so fast that commanders have no time to understand or respond to what their weapons are doing— leaving devastation in their wake.

On the Russian Border

Imagine the following scenario, one among many nightmarish confrontations that could accidentally transpire—unless the race toward AWSs can be stopped. It is 2040, and thousands of autonomous supertanks glisten with frost along Russia's border with Europe. Packs of autonomous supersonic robot jets fly overhead, scouring for enemy activity. Suddenly a tank fires a missile over the horizon, and a civilian airliner goes down in flames. It is an accident—a sensor glitch triggered a confrontation mode—but the tanks do not know that. They rumble forward en masse toward the border. The fighter planes shift into battle formation and send alerts to fleets of robot ships and shoals of autonomous submarines in the Black, Barents and White Seas.

After less than 10 seconds, NATO's autonomous counterweapons swoop in from the air, and attack formations begin to develop on the ground and in the sea. Each side's combat algorithms are unknown to its enemy, so no one can predict how the opposing forces will interact. The fighter jets avoid one another by swooping, diving and twisting with centrifugal forces that would kill any human, and they communicate among themselves at machine speeds. Each side has many tricks up its sleeve for gaming the other. These include disrupting each other's signals and spoofing with fake GPS coordinates to upset coordination and control.

Within three minutes hundreds of jets are fighting in the skies over Russian and European cities at near-hypersonic speed. The tanks have burst across the border and are firing on communications infrastructure, as well as at all moving vehicles at railway stations and on roads. Large guns on autonomous ships are pounding the land. Autonomous naval battles have broken out on and under the seas. Military leaders on both sides are trying to make sense of the devastation that is happening around them. But what can they do? All communications with the weapons have been jammed, and there is a complete breakdown of command-and-control structures. Only 22 minutes have passed since the accidental shooting-down of the airliner, and swarms of tanks are fast approaching Helsinki, Tallinn, Riga, Vilnius, Kyiv and Tbilisi.

Russian and Western leaders begin urgent discussions, but no one can work out how this started or why. Fingers are itching on nuclear buttons as near-futile efforts are underway to evacuate the major cities. There is no precedent for this chaos, and the militaries are befuddled. Their planning has fallen apart, and the death toll is ramping up by the millisecond. Navigation systems have been widely spoofed, so some of the weapons are breaking from the swarms and crashing into buildings. Others have been hacked and are going on killing sprees. False electronic signals are making weapons fire at random. The countryside is littered with the bodies of animals and humans; cities lie in ruins.

The Importance of Humans

A binding international treaty to prohibit the development, production and use of AWSs and to ensure meaningful human control over weapons systems becomes more urgent every day. A human expert, with full awareness of the situation and context and with sufficient time to deliberate on the nature, significance and legitimacy of the targets, the necessity and appropriateness of an attack and the likely outcomes, should determine whether or not the attack will commence. For the past six years the Campaign to Stop Killer Robots has been trying to persuade the member states of the U.N. to agree on a treaty. We work at the U.N. Convention on Certain Conventional Weapons (CCW), a forum of 125 nations for negotiating bans on weapons that cause undue suffering. Thousands of scientists and leaders in the fields of computing and machine learning have joined this call, and so have many companies, such as Google's DeepMind. At last count, 30 nations had demanded an outright ban of fully autonomous weapons, but most others want regulations to ensure that humans are responsible for making the decision to attack (or not). Progress is being blocked, however, by a small handful of nations led by the U.S., Russia, Israel and Australia.

At the CCW, Russia and the U.S. have made it clear that they are opposed to the term "human control." The U.S. is striving to replace it with "appropriate levels of human judgment"—which could mean no human control at all, if that were deemed appropriate. Fortunately, some hope still exists. U.N. Secretary-General António Guterres informed the group of governmental experts at the CCW that "machines with the power and discretion to take lives without human involvement are politically unacceptable, are morally repugnant and should be prohibited by international law." Common sense and humanity must prevail—before it is too late.

Referenced

Towards a Principle for the Human Supervisory Control of Robot Weapons. Noel Sharkey in *Politica & Società*, No. 2, pages 305–324; 2014.

Measuring Autonomous Weapon Systems against International Humanitarian Law Rules. Thompson Chengeta in *Journal of Law and Cyber Warfare*, Vol. 5, pages 63–137; Summer 2016.

Algorithms Delegated with Life and Death Decisions. Noel Sharkey in *Revue Defense Nationale*, No. 820, pages 173–178; May 2019.

About the Author

Noel Sharkey is professor emeritus of artificial intelligence and robotics at the University of Sheffield in England. He is a founder and chair of the International Committee for Robot Arms Control.

Here's How to End the Fog of Cyber War

By The Editors of *Scientific American*

The world is at war. Some might quibble with the characterization of malicious hacking as warfare, preferring phrases such as "cyberespionage" or "cyberconflict." But when governments, industry and individuals are under constant attack by antagonists from all corners of the globe—marauders who use the Internet to steal vital information, sabotage critical operations and recruit terrorists—this means war. It is high time for an internationally coordinated response.

The first skirmish arguably took place in 2007, when online attacks against the Baltic state of Estonia took down critical government, banking and media Web sites. Suspicion soon fell on state-sponsored Russian hackers retaliating against Estonia's removal of a Soviet-era war memorial from the center of the country's capital, Tallinn. The use of proxy servers and spoofed Internet addresses to route the attacks, however, made it very difficult to trace their source, and the Russian government has denied any involvement.

Subsequent international incidents have followed a similar attack-and-deny pattern. The Kremlin has never admitted to launching or sanctioning cyberattacks against Georgian media, communications and transportation companies in advance of Russia's 2008 ground war against that country. Nor has the U.S. officially taken responsibility for the Stuxnet or Duqu malware attacks on Iran from 2007 to 2011, which damaged centrifuges crucial to the country's nuclear program—despite reports that U.S. and Israeli programmers developed those cyberweapons.

Cyberattacks have only escalated since then. The obscure, hard-to-trace origins of these assaults not only protect the guilty party (or parties) from law-enforcement agencies or retaliation, they also create paranoia that puts a strain on international diplomatic relations.

It is difficult to penalize or hit back at an enemy when you aren't sure who it is. In 2015 China emerged as the most likely culprit after the U.S. Office of Personnel Management discovered the theft of more than 21.5 million data records from its computer systems. China's denials, however, set up a familiar stalemate—until the Obama administration threatened to levy economic sanctions against Chinese firms that benefited from the hacking of any U.S. entities.

This change of tactics—targeting the results of a cyberattack rather than the source—helped to bring U.S. and Chinese presidents Barack Obama and Xi Jinping to the bargaining table in late September. The two leaders promised, among other things, that neither the U.S. nor the Chinese government would target each other for economic espionage via the Internet and that their countries would cooperate during cybercrime investigations. U.S. and Chinese officials continue to work out the details. A key aspect, of course, is figuring out how this pact will be enforced.

Other countries and international entities are pushing similar agendas aimed at creating a cybertruce. The U.S., China, Russia and several other world powers pledged not to engage in cyberespionage for economic benefit following the Group of 20 conference last November. Members of the U.S. House Intelligence Committee have called on the country's intelligence community to help create international rules of online engagement, which they refer to as an "E-Neva Convention." The United Nations and NATO have likewise weighed in with rules that would prohibit states from intentionally damaging one another's critical infrastructure and from interfering with national emergency response teams defending against cyberattacks.

It will take more than pledges and frameworks, however. These proposals must be legally binding treaties that include fines, penalties and other enforceable mechanisms. They need to actively discourage online aggression and hold nations responsible for misuse of the Internet infrastructure they provide or support. This last part is particularly important because so many cyberattacks against government computers come from shadowy groups acting independently of any nation or state.

A certain degree of cyberconflict is inevitable, but the establishment of international rules of online conduct and penalties for noncompliance is vital to suppress the worst of it.

Here's What a Cyber Warfare Arsenal Might Look Like

By Larry Greenemeier

The Pentagon has made clear in recent weeks that cyber warfare is no longer just a futuristic threat—it is now a real one. U.S. government agency and industry computer systems are already embroiled in a number of nasty cyber warfare campaigns against attackers based in China, North Korea, Russia and elsewhere. As a counterpoint, hackers with ties to Russia have been accused of stealing a number of Pres. Barack Obama's e-mails, although the White House has not formally blamed placed any blame at the Kremlin's doorstep. The Obama administration did, however, call out North Korea for ordering last year's cyber attack on Sony Pictures Entertainment.

The battle has begun. "External actors probe and scan [U.S. Department of Defense (DoD)] networks for vulnerabilities millions of times each day, and over 100 foreign intelligence agencies continually attempt to infiltrate DoD networks," Eric Rosenbach, assistant secretary for homeland defense and global security, testified in April before the U.S. Senate Committee on Armed Services, Subcommittee on Emerging Threats and Capabilities. "Unfortunately, some incursions—by both state and nonstate entities—have succeeded."

After years of debate as to how the fog of war will extend to the Internet, in April 2015 Obama signed an executive order declaring cyber attacks launched from abroad against U.S. targets a "national emergency" and levying sanctions against those responsible. Penalties include freezing the U.S. assets of cyber attackers and those aiding them as well as preventing U.S. residents from conducting financial transactions with those targeted by the executive order.

Deterrence of this type can only go so far, of course, which is why the DoD last month issued an updated version of its cyber strategy for engaging its adversaries online. The plan outlines Defense's efforts to shore up government networks, systems and information as well as those run by U.S. companies.

If cyber attacks continue to increase at the current rate, they could destabilize already tense world situations, says O. Sami Saydjari, a former Pentagon cyber expert who now runs a consultancy called the Cyber Defense Agency. "Nations must begin to create real consequences for malicious action in cyberspace because they are leading, in aggregate, to serious damage, and there is potential for much larger damage than we have seen so far," he adds.

A major part of the DoD's cyber strategy is to bolster the Pentagon's "cyber mission force," which the department began forming in 2013 to carry out its operations in cyberspace. Although the unit will not be fully operational before 2018 the unit is expected to have nearly 6,200 military, civilian and contractors—divided into 13 teams—working across various military departments and defense agencies to "hunt down online intruders," Defense Secretary Ashton Carter said last month during a lecture delivered at Stanford University.

The strategy does not go into detail about which digital weapons the cyber mission force will deploy to fight its campaigns. That information can instead be gleaned from the malicious software—"malware"—already rampant on the Internet as well as military technologies designed to disrupt digital communications. The Stuxnet worm that sabotaged Iran's Natanz uranium enrichment plant in November 2007 is an early example of cyber war weaponry. No one has officially claimed ownership of Stuxnet although much speculation points to the U.S. and Israel as its authors. A related piece of strategic malware known as Flame is subtler, stealthily gathering information and transmitting it via Bluetooth while avoiding detection.

The components of cyber warfare are the very same components as warfare using guns and explosives, only much faster, Saydjari says. An attacker would seek to damage a critical infrastructure such as power, telecommunications or banking by damaging the computer systems that control those infrastructures. "The instrument of creating that damage is generally some form of malicious software that is inserted into such systems by a variety of means including hacking into the system by taking advantage of some known but as yet unpatched or as yet undiscovered vulnerability," he adds.

China recently admitted that it has both military and civilian teams of programmers developing digital weapons, and documents disclosed by National Security Agency whistle-blower Edward Snowden indicate China has developed malware to attack U.S. Defense Department computers and even steal sensitive information about the F-35 Lightning II fighter plane that Lockheed Martin is developing for the U.S. Air Force. "All technically savvy countries are developing both offensive and defensive capabilities to prepare for the potential of cyber conflict both by itself and as one aspect of broader conflicts including kinetic warfare, which involves bombs and bullets," Saydjari says. "The goal of many such countries is to be able to exercise complete dominance and control over any part of cyberspace, anywhere and anytime it serves their national interests."

The Air Force Research Laboratory is soliciting projects that could furnish cyber deception capabilities for use by commanders to "provide false information, confuse, delay or otherwise impede cyber attackers to the benefit of friendly forces." Another aspect of cyber warfare could be the use of cyber electromagnetic activities to "seize, retain and exploit an advantage over adversaries and enemies in both cyberspace and the electromagnetic spectrum," according to a U.S. Army report on the subject. Electromagnetic attacks have already struck in South Korea where more than 500 aircraft flying in and out of that country's Incheon and Gimpo airports reported GPS failures in 2010, *IEEE Spectrum* reported in 2014. The source of the electromagnetic fields was traced to the North Korean city of Kaesong, about 50 kilometers north of Incheon.

Cyber war itself may be difficult to define but cyber treaties pose an even bigger challenge. "In some sense it is a bit like asking bank robbers in the old wild West to negotiate a non–bank-robbing treaty," Saydjari says. "Many countries are benefiting from the lack of rules. Many countries are exploring this new arena of warfare and do not quite understand it well enough to agree to stop exploring it."

Even more importantly, he adds, it is very difficult to attribute responsibility to actions within cyberspace because of its complexity, "so imposing consequences to treaty violation would be problematic."

About the Author

Larry Greenemeier is the associate editor of technology for Scientific American, *covering a variety of tech-related topics, including biotech, computers, military tech, nanotech and robots.*

Section 2: Infrastructure Under Attack

2.1   Hacker Attack on Essential Pipeline Shows Infrastructure
       Weaknesses
         By Sophie Bushwick

2.2   How Hackers Tried to Add Dangerous Lye into a City's
       Water Supply
         By Sophie Bushwick

2.3   Is the Power Grid Getting More Vulnerable to Cyber Attacks?
         By Jesse Dunietz

2.4   The Most Vulnerable Ransomware Targets Are the Institutions
       We Rely On Most
         By Annie Sneed

2.5   U.S. Hospitals Not Immune to Crippling Cyber Attacks
         By Dina Fine Maron

2.6   Urban Bungle: Atlanta Cyber Attack Puts Other Cities on Notice
         By Larry Greenemeier

2.7   What Do Hurricanes and Cybersecurity Have in Common?
         By Algirde Pipikaite, Haiyan Song

Hacker Attack on Essential Pipeline Shows Infrastructure Weaknesses

By Sophie Bushwick

A crucial U.S. fuel pipeline operator recently announced it had been hit by ransomware, a type of cyberattack in which hackers encrypt important data so their owners cannot access them—unless the owners pay the criminals to unlock the information. Colonial Pipeline, a private company that transports nearly half of the U.S. East Coast's gasoline and other fuel, had to shut down 5,500 miles of its fuel pipeline as a result. The FBI has blamed the attack on a criminal group called DarkSide.

Unlike ransomware used to kidnap an individual's computer files, lock up a university's network or extort a hospital, attacks on major infrastructure such as Colonial Pipeline's fuel pipeline can have enormous impacts on whole regions of the country. DarkSide's ransomware "caused a fairly significant disruption to the fuel supply across the East Coast and caused a number of policy interventions and reactions from the administration [of President Joe Biden] about trying to make it easier to transport fuel and mitigate the impacts of that," says Josephine Wolff, an assistant professor of cybersecurity policy at Tufts University. *Scientific American* spoke with Wolff about the threat posed by ransomware, how vulnerable the U.S.'s critical infrastructure really is—and what can be done to protect it.

[An edited transcript of the interview follows.]

Q: Are ransomware attacks becoming more frequent?
A: It's hard to pin down really good numbers because [there are] a lot of ransomware attacks we don't hear about publicly. There's no requirement to report them, most of the time. But the ones we hear about are clearly becoming not just more numerous but also more significant in their impacts. If we think back a couple of years, we had the city of Atlanta, the city of Baltimore,

a number of public government-focused attacks that were using ransomware. More recently there's been a lot of focus on the attacks aimed at hospitals and health care providers. And looming in the background, though we've seen fewer examples of it, has been the threat of attacks like this: targeting critical infrastructure that would significantly disrupt operations and daily life.

Q: Other than pipelines, what other types of infrastructure are at risk?

A: The typical example that people use is the electric grid. What happens if somebody is able to prevent the provision of electricity across some part of the country? The Colonial Pipeline shutdown, though it's not exactly that, fits into that nightmare scenario of "What do we do if we lose control over our power infrastructure?" But it's true across a number of critical infrastructure sectors. What happens if a large part of the banking infrastructure is shut down or impossible to access? What happens if the subway system in a major city is compromised, and it's impossible to schedule trains or operate transportation? Up until this point, mostly, we've just been imagining these scenarios. There have been a few high-profile examples of the power sector being targeted, but this is still a fairly rare occurrence—and, for that reason, quite striking.

Q: Are these systems adequately protected?

A: The general answer is that probably nothing in our energy sector is being adequately protected. It's a sector with an enormous number of legacy systems and complicated infrastructure, and it's a sector that always has to be up and running. So it's not easy to say, "We're going to take a week or a month or a year and completely revamp everything and update all the systems."

Q: How can these potential targets better defend themselves?

A: They should be, first of all, really trying to lock down their perimeter defenses—which is to say all of the security controls that they use to try and prevent malware from being delivered to their computers in the first place. That could be things such as two-factor authentication, e-mail warnings for external mail, and screening of new USB drives or other devices that are plugged into your system. I think there should be a lot of controls (especially right now, at a moment when a lot of people are working from home) around remote access—the computers that are connecting to your system from outside your offices.

A big [defense] is what we would call network segmentation: making sure that if one piece of a company's infrastructure is compromised and targeted, it's very, very difficult to spread that malware across the larger network. One of the things that is pretty striking about this story is that the Colonial Pipeline has shut down more than 5,000 miles of pipeline. That, to me, suggests either that a very large swath of its system has been compromised or that [the company is] worried that it very easily could be. Ideally, you would not have that large an impact from one initial compromise.

Another piece is thinking about how you get systems back up and running very quickly, because when you're dealing with critical infrastructure, you don't have a lot of time to take everything off-line. There's a lot of rapid decision-making that needs to happen. There's a lot to be said for trying to run some test drills and making sure that there's a really clear plan in place for a situation like this. I also think that's part of discouraging ransoms—to make people feel like "We've trained for this; we know what to do," as opposed to "We've never seen anything like this. I guess we have to pay."

Q: Beyond individual systems, what should the government do to help?

A: I would like to see a much more forceful prohibition on the payment of most ransoms. That's my opinion; that's not everybody's opinion. But what is it that the U.S. government can do unilaterally? Trying to make this a less profitable endeavor, long term, is one of the most effective measures that we could try to implement. [Cracking] down on how easily those ransoms are paid, how easily they're covered by insurers, I think, could make a big difference in terms of how much money these criminals can make—and therefore how many of them are entering the business and using this as a way to profit.

Q: What do we know about these criminals? Just how profitable is the ransomware industry?

A: We know it's profitable because we know people continue to do it, and that's actually the strongest indication we have that people are continuing to make money. But exactly how much money they're making is very hard to estimate meaningfully. The group that the Colonial Pipeline ransomware has been attributed to is a criminal organization that is very focused on ransomware as a service—making ransomware tools and code available to customers to direct their own attacks. That matters because this organization, DarkSide, is building this business not just as a way to target companies but also as a way to make it easier for other criminals. That—again, without having hard data—speaks a little bit to the scale of this problem.

Q: Would we have more hard data if victims were required to report ransomware attacks?

A: Having a reporting requirement would, at the very least, help us get a better handle on the size and scale of the problem. When we make these statements like "Ransomware is on the rise" or "2021 is the worst year for ransomware yet," we would actually have some harder data behind those kinds of generalizations. But I also think it would give us a lot more insight into: What are the criminals' profit margins? Who's paying them? How much is being paid? How do we make ransomware a less profitable endeavor?

About the Author

Sophie Bushwick is an associate editor covering technology at Scientific American.

How Hackers Tried to Add Dangerous Lye into a City's Water Supply

By Sophie Bushwick

O n February 5, an unknown cyberattacker tried to poison the water supply of Oldsmar, Fla. City officials say the targeted water-treatment facility had a software remote-access system that let staff control the plant's computers from a distance. The hacker entered the system and set it to massively increase sodium hydroxide levels in the water. This chemical (better known as lye) was originally set at 100 parts per million, an innocuous amount that helps control the water's pH levels. The attacker tried to boost that to 11,100 ppm, high enough to damage skin and cause hair loss if the water contacts the body—or, if it is ingested, to cause potentially deadly gastrointestinal symptoms. Fortunately, a staff member noticed the attack as it was happening and restored the correct settings before anything changed.

How much of a broader threat might attacks like this pose to public facilities, and what can be done to protect them? *Scientific American* asked Ben Buchanan, a professor specializing in cybersecurity and statecraft at Georgetown University's School of Foreign Service.

[An edited transcript of the interview follows.]

Q: What might make city infrastructure like a water treatment plant vulnerable to hackers?

A: Speaking generally, the challenge with a lot of these facilities is oftentimes that they are older, or they just don't have the security infrastructure that we would want to guard against hackers. So, if the systems are not as secure as we would like, but their internet is accessible, that is a recipe for trouble.

Q: Who might have been responsible for the attack?

A: Oftentimes the thing about targeting an industrial control system is that, in order to have the effect you want as an attacker, you need to understand the system reasonably well. If you're truly a foreign attacker, you want to do a lot of reconnaissance on the system. If you're an insider, you already have that kind of knowledge. A lot of times the people who carry out cases like this—of which there are not that many—were disgruntled employees who already knew the system and how to manipulate it. [But in this case] it is too soon to say, 'This is a disgruntled employee,' and it's definitely too soon to say, 'Oh, this is Iran or Russia and it's a clear act of war.' The speculation doesn't help right now.

Q: Oldsmar is a small city with a population of 15,000. Does that make it less of a target, or is it actually more vulnerable compared to a plant in a larger, more populated area?

A: I don't know that it generalizes one way or the other. If it's an insider, then that explains why they're targeting that facility—but we don't know that. I think it probably stands to reason that foreign hackers who want to make a big splash would choose a bigger target. But on the other hand, we have a case from a couple of years ago in which Iranian hackers were indicted by the U.S. government for breaking into the computer networks of this old dam that no one really was using much anymore.

Q: The hacker gained access through an existing software program that enables remote access of the plant's computers. Should that type of program be prohibited for plants like this?

A: It'd be hard in the COVID moment to say, "Everything's got to be managed on-site." I don't know how realistic that is. But I think balancing the security and usability of these systems is often hard. Getting the balance right often depends on more resources than a lot of these facilities have.

Q: How should facilities like these be protecting themselves?

A: One thing that's really important is to have redundancy in systems, especially around safety systems. There's an important distinction here between security and safety. Cybersecurity is keeping the bad actors out of the computer networks, or limiting what they can do once they're inside the computer networks. Technically, safety is making sure the industrial control systems' components don't do anything that puts people at risk, even if they're given instructions to do that—by hackers or by somebody else. For example, one thing you have is: Are there mechanisms in place to regularly test the processes and the outputs of an industrial control system, to test the particular qualities of the water? Are there people who are monitoring systems to make sure that things don't move out of whack for unclear reasons?

In that respect, this is at least somewhat of a success story. Because although there was intent to attack here, and there was action to attack here, no one was harmed. I think you want to have those levels of redundancy any time you're dealing with critical systems like those in industrial control. In my second book I wrote about (depending on how you count) four attacks on industrial control systems, all of which were far more significant than this. So, this doesn't reach the level of attacks that were more successful.

Q: What can we learn from this?

A: The case shows that there are bad actors out there, that money and time we spend securing and making safe our industrial control systems is often money and time well spent—but that we can actually manage to defend the systems in such a way that (against at least some attacks) minimizes the amount of harm that's done.

Q: So, people shouldn't be panicking about their water right now?

A: I think that there's certainly no reason nationwide to panic. This is a reminder of the importance of the work of industrial control systems professionals, and the people who secure those systems. But there's no reason to overhype what happened here and spin it as "the sky is falling" when, in fact, the sky is not falling.

About the Author

Sophie Bushwick is an associate editor covering technology at Scientific American.

Is the Power Grid Getting More Vulnerable to Cyber Attacks?

By Jesse Dunietz

In August 2017 it was cyberattacks on the Irish power grid. In July it was a digital assault on U.S. energy companies, including a nuclear power plant. Back in December 2016 a Russian hack of a Vermont utility was all over the news. From the media buzz, one might conclude that power grid infrastructure is teetering on the brink of a hacker-induced meltdown.

The real story is more nuanced, however. *Scientific American* spoke with grid cybersecurity expert Robert M. Lee, CEO of industrial cybersecurity firm Dragos, Inc., to sort out fact from hype. Dragos, which aims to protect critical infrastructure from cyberattacks, recently raised $10 million from investors to further its mission. Before he founded the company, Lee worked for the U.S. government analyzing and defending against cyberattacks on infrastructure. For a portion of his military career, he also worked on the government's offensive front. His work has given him a front-row view on both sides of infrastructure cybersecurity.

[An edited transcript of the interview follows.]

Q: How concerned should we be about grid and infrastructure cybersecurity, and what should we be most worried about?

A: The electric grid and most infrastructure we have is actually fairly well built for reliability and safety. We've had a strong safety culture in industrial engineering for decades. That safety and reliability has never been thought of from a cybersecurity perspective, but it has afforded us a very defensible environment.

As an example: if a portion of the U.S. power grid goes down. We usually anticipate those things for hurricanes or winter-weather storms. And we're good at moving away from the computers and doing manual operations, just working the infrastructure to get it back. Usually it's hours, maybe days; never more than a week or so.

A lot of these cyberattacks deal with the computer technology and the interconnected nature of the infrastructure. And so when they target it in that way, you're talking hours, maybe a day, at most a week of disruption. For reasonable scenarios, we're not talking about a long time of outages, and we're not talking about compromising safety.

Now, the scary side of it is [twofold]. One, our adversaries are getting much more aggressive. They're learning a lot about our industrial systems, not just from a computer technology standpoint but from an industrial engineering standpoint, thinking about how to disrupt or maybe even destroy equipment. That's where you start reaching some particularly alarming scenarios.

The second thing is, a lot of that ability to return to manual operation, the rugged nature of our infrastructure—a lot of that's changing. Because of business reasons, because of lack of people to man the jobs, we're starting to see more and more computer-based systems. We're starting to see more common operating platforms. And this facilitates a scale for adversaries that they couldn't previously get.

Q: When you say our adversaries are getting more aggressive, what are you referring to?

A: The key events are things like the Ukraine attack in 2015–2016, [in which a cyberattack brought down portions of the Ukrainian power grid], as well as two different campaigns in 2013–2014, BlackEnergy2 and Havex, [two malware programs that were deployed against energy sector companies]. Basically, far-reaching espionage on industrial facilities one year; the next year getting into industrial environments; and then culmination in attacks in 2015–2016. That's aggressive in itself.

For my own firm, what we're seeing in the [overall] activity in the space is it's growing. Over the last decade, I have seen adversary activity increase in some measure, and then around 2013–2014 just start spiking.

Q: What are the adversaries actually doing in these attacks?

A: [There are two broad categories of attacks.] Stage I intrusions are those designed to gain information. These are the traditional espionage efforts we've become accustomed to hearing about, where information is stolen or deleted. A Stage II attack could result in temporary loss of power, physical damage to equipment, or other types of scenarios we often hear about. It is important to note these are not trivial to accomplish. If an attacker wants to progress to a Stage II attack, during the Stage I intrusion they have to steal information specific to [that] industrial environment.

The 2013–2014 campaigns that I mentioned were exactly the kinds of Stage I activity that you'd want to use to pivot into a Stage II activity. And so they scared the heck out of all of us. But the stuff we've heard about recently—the nuclear site and about a dozen energy companies that were compromised in a phishing campaign that made the news—none of that sounded tailored toward pivoting into a Stage II.

Q: Once an adversary has broken into the "business networks" used for email, documents and so on, how far a jump is it for them to access the industrial control system (ICS) networks used to control and monitor the industrial equipment?

A: In nuclear environments, [business networks and control networks are] airgapped—[i.e., computers on one network cannot talk to those on the other]—because of safety regulations. The idea that because you got into the business network you can easily move into the ICS network is ridiculous. That is not true with other industrial infrastructures—electric energy, oil and gas, manufacturing, etc. You absolutely have [ICS] networks that are connected up.

The nuance here is that we have a joke in the community: you'll get security folks who don't know much about ICS coming in with penetration testers and saying, "Oh my gosh, I found so many vulnerabilities!" And so the joke is, why don't I just sit you down at the terminal? I will give you 100 percent access. Now make the lights blink. There's a big gap there. [So the challenge is] not so much getting access. It's once you get access, do you know what to do in a way that's not just going to be embarrassing?

Q: What motivation do these adversaries have to attack the U.S. grid?

A: I do not feel that there is a legitimate reason for adversaries to disrupt or destroy industrial infrastructure outside of a conflict scenario. Ukraine and Russia is a great example. I don't necessarily mean declared war, but in places where we see conflict, I think we'll see industrial attacks: North Korea-South Korea, China-Taiwan.

But there are some scenarios that concern me, where we might have our hands forced and not have clarity around what happened. I'm aware of at least one case where a skilled adversary broke into an industrial environment, and in the course of intelligence operations they accidentally knocked over some sensitive system that led to visible destruction and almost to multiple casualties. And the worst part is, we didn't actually realize it was a failed operation until about a month after, because the forensics and analysis take time. So you could have a scenario where the U.S., Russia, China, Iran—big players—are doing intelligence operations on each other, are doing pre-positioning to have deterrence or political leverage, and mess up that operation in a way that looks like an attack that we do not have transparency on for some time. We do not have international norms around how to handle that.

Outside of conflict scenarios, though, I don't see the advantage to [deliberate] disruptive or destructive attacks. I think we haven't seen it not because they haven't wanted to, but because the return on investment is minimal. What's really advantageous is sitting U.S. congressmen and policymakers fearing what can happen with industrial infrastructure. That fear drives policy far more than actually turning the lights off and having them realize [they will] come back on in six hours.

Q: What should we be doing to improve robustness against cyberattacks?

A: There's a sliding scale of [security measures] you can invest in. You have architecture—building it right from the beginning. Next is passive defense: vendor tools and security tools on top of the architecture. On top of that is active defense—people hunting inside the environment for threats. On top of that is intelligence, which is analysis of adversary campaigns and maybe even breaking into their networks. Then there's offense, which is obviously some sort of attack, maybe to take down malicious infrastructure.

I've long maintained that the security community is positioned toward the offensive side of the scale because it sounds cooler. But the most value for organizations is on the other side.

Our regulations and our industry trends have gotten our architecture to a pretty decent place. The passive defenses probably need some work, but we're getting there. The piece that is completely lacking is active defense. There are less than 1,000 ICS cybersecurity professionals worldwide. We've got to focus on training the human. The only way to counter human adversaries that are flexible and funded is with trained defenders operating in defensible environments.

In both the Ukraine attacks, and even in Stuxnet, [the attack on Iranian uranium refineries in 2010], they're very obvious on the network. We just have environments where people aren't looking or don't have the technology to give them insight. Once we have environments that facilitate people asking questions, and we have people [who] ask the right questions, we'll find that defenders actually have a pretty strong upper hand in this field.

About the Author

Jesse Dunietz is a computer scientist and the Technology, Energy, and Society Fellow at Securing America's Future Energy (SAFE).

The Most Vulnerable Ransomware Targets Are the Institutions We Rely On Most

By Annie Sneed

I n 2016 a Los Angeles hospital became yet another victim of ransomware—a type of cyber attack where hackers encrypt data on individuals' or institutions' computers and demand a ransom to unlock the information. A few weeks later the Los Angeles County Department of Health Services reportedly suffered a similar fate. These are just two cases in a rising tide of ransomware hacks, and experts predict the problem is only going to get worse. Unfortunately, it turns out that some of easiest ransomware attack targets are the critical establishments that we rely on most.

Many vital public institutions such as hospitals, police stations and fire stations typically do not have the most sophisticated cybersecurity, and they are perhaps the most vulnerable of all in ransomware attacks. This is not because public institutions are more exposed to these attacks than, say, restaurants or dentists—the problem is that there is more at stake for everyone when these institutions become victims.

Ransomware has been around since the late 1980s, but in recent years it has become increasingly popular with cyber criminals, especially since the creation of bitcoin in 2009 gave hackers an easy way to get paid anonymously. In 2014 ransomware attacks rose 113 percent compared with the previous year, and 2015 estimates also show rapid growth, says Kevin Haley, director of Symantec Security Response. Ransomware hackers trick victims into visiting an infected Web site or downloading an attachment and then encrypt their data. Hackers post a ransom note on a user's screen; if the victim does not pay within a certain amount of time, their data is lost forever.

Criminals like ransomware because it works. "This software is very effective at getting money out of people," explains Justin Cappos, a computer security expert at New York University. The hackers usually demand fairly small payment of a few hundred dollars, so they tend to fly under law enforcement's radar. But they target so many people that they can take in millions. "It's a volume business, like McDonald's," explains Phil Lieberman, founder of Lieberman Software and a cybersecurity expert. Although ransomware attacks are mostly random, researchers say that cybercriminals have found a "sweet spot" of $10,000 when they specifically target businesses—a big sum, but still low enough that it will not attract too much attention from law enforcement.

Some groups are prepared to deal with this threat. Tech companies, financial firms and certain government agencies tend to have to have sophisticated cybersecurity to help them fend off attacks and recover quickly when they happen. But small and midsize businesses, including mom-and-pop shops, restaurants, dentists and attorneys are typically less well protected, as are crucial public institutions.

Many police stations, for example, have had their data held hostage by hackers. In 2013 ransomware struck the Swansea Police Department in Massachusetts and encrypted its main file server, locking up important administrative and investigative documents as well as seven years' of mug shots. The department paid $750 to get its data back. Similar attacks were launched on police stations from Tennessee to Maine to Chicago. Fire departments have also been victims of ransomware. In 2015 a Maryland fire department reportedly had to shut down its computerized dispatch center and record everything on paper because of an attack. Ransomware is especially troublesome for these kinds of institutions because they absolutely need to get that critical data back to continue operating.

Like police and fire stations, hospitals are vulnerable because they also run 24/7 and also have irreplaceable data. Yet hospitals may actually be more susceptible to ransomware attacks for reasons unique to the medical industry. Some medical institutions use old legacy administrative software that only works on outdated operating systems, which contain more weaknesses for ransomware to exploit. It is also difficult for hospitals to update software on medical devices because of tight regulations, and this leaves them more open to attacks as well. "You can't just roll out new software," explains Josephine Wolff, a computing security expert at the Rochester Institute of Technology, "The medical world is dealing with a very complicated legal and policy regime around medical data and how it has to be handled."

Critical infrastructure, such as dams, power grids and other systems are increasingly linked to the Internet, meaning they, too, are exposed to ransomware. "We're getting more and more connected in ways that developers of these systems did not envision many years ago," explains Engin Kirda, a professor of computer science at Northeastern University. "As a result, these systems could be taken down by malware attacks, and the consequences can be difficult to predict." Experts, however, say that ransomware is less likely to cause major problems for infrastructure than other types of malware because it deals with data rather than interfering with control systems. But Kirda says that, theoretically, ransomware hackers could access certain data that may affect, say, how power is managed. Lieberman agrees: "It's not inconceivable that an attacker could target an employee of a critical infrastructure company, shut down that company down, and demand a ransom to restore access."

Ransomware attacks not only place a financial burden on victims, they also hinder the operations of these crucial public institutions. In the case of the Los Angeles hospital it took $17,000 (40 bitcoins) in payment and 10 days before the hospital had its system running again. And although paying the hackers may seem like a relatively small price compared with losing all that data, experts say there is more at stake. The cash that institutions, businesses and average citizens send to hackers ends up in bad places. "The money goes to criminal organizations and a lot of them are involved in really despicable things like human trafficking," Cappos says. "You're really providing funding and support to people doing horrible things." And when victims show they're willing to pay, it attracts more criminals to the ransomware market.

Experts encourage everyone—from police stations to corporations to individuals—to follow best security practices. Most importantly: have backups. "Ransomware relies on the idea that hackers have managed to encrypt something that's really valuable to you because you only have one copy," Wolff explains. "If you have backups, then what they've got has no value."

About the Author

Annie Sneed is a science journalist who has written for the New York Times, Wired, *Public Radio International and* Fast Company.

U.S. Hospitals Not Immune to Crippling Cyber Attacks

By Dina Fine Maron

Hospitals and medical devices in the U.S. are extremely vulnerable to the type of massive cyber attack that tore through more than 150 countries Friday, and some health care providers here may have already been—or soon will be—hit, cybersecurity analysts warn.

The attack relied on a type of malicious software called ransomware, which keeps users from accessing their computer systems until they pay a ransom. The pernicious new strain, aptly named WannaCry, froze or slowed business and health care computer systems around the world, including several within the U.K.'s National Health Service.

The malware exploits a vulnerability in the Windows operating system that many system administrators have not yet patched—including at many U.S. hospitals, experts warn. Moreover, WannaCry does not distinguish between a computer, smartphone or medical device. And, unlike the case with many other cyber attacks, a user need not click a link to unknowingly install it; if a health care system is connected to the internet and using an outdated system, the malware can find it and infect it.

"It's kind of like we closed our doors but left them unlocked, so the malware just wiggles doorknobs until it finds one that's open and walks in. You don't need to be there to get robbed," says Kevin Fu, CEO and chief scientist of health care security company Virta Labs and director of the Archimedes Center for Medical Devices at the University of Michigan. "We know the vulnerability is out there for U.S. hospitals" because many of its health care facilities have outdated systems, he says.

In a hospital setting, a WannaCry infection can cause serious problems including blocking access to patient records and lab results or a failure to share allergy or drug interaction information with hospital computers or other devices. A user may only discover the security breach after turning on a device, when a locked screen comes up stating the person's data is being held hostage unless a ransom is paid. The ransom fees (reportedly between $300 and $600) are apparently designed to be low enough to incentivize payment.

No hospital or other medical organization in U.S. had publicly reported a WannaCry attack as of the beginning of this week. Exactly why—or even if—hospitals and medical systems here have avoided the latest malware attack remains unknown. The U.S. health care system is less centralized than the U.K.'s, which may have provided some degree of insulation, says Alex Heid, chief research officer at SecurityScorecard, a risk management cybersecurity firm that tracks cyber attacks on health care in the U.S. Still, Heid warns U.S. health care providers' computer networks may already be under assault from threats that are not widely known. "It is likely that [WannaCry] just didn't hit a large network of our sites—the equivalent of NHS—but I guarantee American systems did get impacted in some regard," he says, noting historically many companies have simply paid small ransoms rather than publicize that they have had glitches.

It is no secret health care providers are worried. One large hospital system in Boston took some drastic steps this weekend, disabling all attachments in e-mails—even though WannaCry can spread without any victim interaction, Fu says. "I would say we had dodged a bullet [compared with the U.K.], but I think the bullets are still coming and we know we are just as vulnerable," he says, noting the malware could be further tweaked to cause future problems.

Cyber attacks against hospital systems are already widespread. Last year Heid's company released an analysis concluding about 75 percent of all major health care providers had experienced malware infections that could cause them to lose data or money. "The American health care system still has a lot of the same problems that would lead to the type of problems we saw in the U.K.," Heid says. "Mainly, there is a lot of legacy software and outdated software that is very prevalent in the medical field."

U.S. government guidance released in July 2016 states that under current health privacy law, health care providers must report malware attacks. But so far that action has not led to a significant increase in reports of incidents, Fu says, citing his own unpublished analysis comparing the number of reports over time. This apparent lack of change, he notes, could suggest that many institutions may still not be reporting attacks.

Like many computer and smartphone users, hospitals and health care systems may opt not to install security patches and fixes because such upgrades could require a system to temporarily go offline or be slowed. Some facilities may not even be aware they are at risk, either because they have no IT department or because different facilities are handling different branches of their systems, Fu says.

But failure to take speedy, comprehensive action puts companies and hospitals at risk. "Once something is connected to the internet and gets infected, it's just a matter of what the attacker wants to do with it: lock it up, break it or sell it to the highest bidder," Heid says. "The most important thing now is, if anyone has been ignoring Windows updates to get them installed." In our interconnected world there is always risk, he notes—but "best practices can make you less of a target—and you don't want to be the lowest-hanging fruit."

About the Author

Dina Fine Maron, formerly an associate editor at Scientific American, *is now a wildlife trade investigative reporter at* National Geographic.

Urban Bungle: Atlanta Cyber Attack Puts Other Cities on Notice

By Larry Greenemeier

S oon after Atlanta City Auditor Amanda Noble logged onto her work computer the morning of March 22, 2018, she knew something was wrong. The icons on her desktop looked different—in some cases replaced with black rectangles—and she noticed many of the files on her desktop had been renamed with "weapologize" or "imsorry" extensions. Noble called the city's chief information security officer to report the problem and left a message. Next, she called the help desk and was put on hold for a while. "At that point, I realized that I wasn't the only one in the office with computer problems," Noble says.

Those computer problems were part of a high-profile "ransomware" cyberattack on the City of Atlanta that has lasted nearly two weeks and has yet to be fully resolved. During that time the metropolis has struggled to recover encrypted data on employees' computers and restore services on the municipal Web site. The criminals initially gave the city seven days to pay about $51,000 in the cryptocurrency bitcoin to get the decryption key for their data. That deadline came and went last week, yet several services remain offline, suggesting the city likely did not pay the ransom. City officials would not comment on the matter when contacted by *Scientific American*.

The Department of Watershed Management, for example, still cannot accept online or telephone payments for water and sewage bills, nor can the Department of Finance issue business licenses through its Web page. The Atlanta Municipal Court has been unable to process ticket payments either online or in person due to the outage and has had to reschedule some of its hearings. The city took down two of its online services voluntarily as a security precaution: the Hartsfield–Jackson Atlanta International Airport wi-fi network and the ability to process service requests via the city's 311 Web site portal, according to Anne Torres, Atlanta's director of communications. Both are now back online, with airport wi-fi restored Tuesday morning.

The ransomware used to attack Atlanta is called SamSam. Like most malicious software it typically enters computer networks through software whose security protections have not been updated. When attackers find vulnerabilities in a network, they use the ransomware to encrypt files there and demand payment to unlock them. Earlier this year attackers used a derivative of SamSam to lock up files at Hancock Regional Hospital in Greenfield, Ind. The health care institution paid nearly $50,000 to retrieve patient data. "The SamSam ransomware used to attack Atlanta is interesting because it gets into a network and spreads to multiple computers before locking them up," says Jake Williams, founder of computer security firm Rendition Infosec. "The victim then has greater incentive to pay a larger ransom in order to regain control of that network of locked computers."

SamSam has been one of the most successful ransomware programs to date, having pulled in an estimated $850,000 in ransom money since it first appeared in late 2015. By comparison, the WannaCry ransomware that made headlines a year ago when it was used to attack European hospitals, telecoms and railways netted about $140,000 in bitcoin.

The city's technology department—Atlanta Information Management (AIM)—contacted local law enforcement, along with the FBI, Department of Homeland Security, Secret Service and independent forensic experts to help assess the damage and investigate the attack. The attackers set up an online payment portal for the city but soon took the site offline after a local television station published a screen shot of the ransom note, which included a link to the bitcoin wallet meant to collect the ransom.

Several clues indicate Atlanta likely did not pay the attackers, Williams says. "Ransomware gangs typically cut off communications once their victims get law enforcement involved," he says. "Atlanta made it clear at a press conference soon after the malware was detected" that they had done so. The length of time it has taken to slowly bring services back online also suggests the cyber criminals abandoned Atlanta without decrypting the city's files, Williams says. "If that's the case, the city's IT staff spent the past week rebuilding Atlanta's online systems using backed-up data that had not been hit by the ransomware," he says, adding that any data not backed up is likely "lost for good."

"If the city had paid the ransom, I would have expected them to bring up systems more quickly than they have done," says Justin Cappos, a professor of computer science and engineering at New York University's Tandon School of Engineering. "Assuming the city did not pay the ransom, their ability to recover their systems at all shows that they at least did a good job backing up their data."

One silver lining in the cloud hanging over Atlanta's computer network—it is unlikely the attackers targeted Atlanta specifically, Williams says. The attackers likely were out on the internet looking for vulnerable computers to attack when they stumbled onto Atlanta's network and the ransomware automatically encrypted its data. That might explain why they attacked Atlanta and then went quiet after law enforcement got involved, he adds. "They weren't necessarily looking to exploit a large city and it wasn't worth possibly getting caught," Williams says. Baltimore officials came to a similar conclusion last week after a ransomware attack took down the city's computer-aided dispatch system for 911 and 311 calls. Baltimore's technology staff attributed the attack to opportunistic hackers who took advantage of inadvertent changes made to a firewall meant to protect the city's network that instead left it vulnerable for about 24 hours.

City Auditor Noble has been using her personal laptop and city-issued mobile phone to do her job since the ransomware struck. As of Tuesday afternoon she had not tried to use her work computer although AIM gave city employees the go-ahead to use their machines last week. As part of the recovery employees were told last Wednesday to reboot their computers and change their passwords, Noble says.

People concerned about ransomware locking up their work or personal computers should back up their data, not just on a network service like Google Drive or Apple's iCloud but on an actual hard disk that can be disconnected from their computer, Cappos says. The ransomware attacks against Atlanta, Baltimore and other municipalities should cause cities to think about whether they would fare any better in the same situation, Williams says, adding, "If it can happen to them, it could happen to you, too."

About the Author

Larry Greenemeier is the associate editor of technology for Scientific American, *covering a variety of tech-related topics, including biotech, computers, military tech, nanotech and robots.*

What Do Hurricanes and Cybersecurity Have in Common?

By Algirde Pipikaite, Haiyan Song

With hurricanes intensifying, it's not hard to imagine this scenario: it's early October and the Weather Channel is extensively covering a hurricane that's going to hit the East Coast of the United States in five days. Right now, it's just a tropical storm somewhere near Cuba. How do we know? Over 100 years ago the international community decided that it was beneficial for all—countries, regions and hemispheres—to share weather-related information and technology to prepare for and tackle potential risks. Even during the most frigid years of the Cold War, the U.S.S.R. and the United States reported weather patterns to each other and the rest of the world.

This is a remarkable example of sustained international cooperation for the greater good, in the interest of making the right decisions about public safety, agriculture, civilian safety, transport and insurance.

What does this have to do with cybersecurity? Everything.

Cyberattacks can sometimes appear to come almost out of nowhere, devastating businesses and crippling all levels of government. But, like extreme weather events, there are warning signs—if one knows where to look for them and whom to inform about any suspicious occurrence. Suspicious activity at an airport in Germany three weeks ago can turn into a full-scale ransomware issue at JFK tomorrow—grounding planes, tanking stock prices and, in a worst case scenario, costing lives. These kinds of cyber challenges will drive the problems of the 21st century.

To protect people and help businesses, executive boards and the global community need to adjust to the new cyber-driven reality; and to take good decisions, executives and the global community need to have accurate and timely data.

Coming from two different perspectives, from the tech industry and international policy, it is clear to us that cyber information sharing between businesses, governments and across borders is the right solution. It can be as effective as the exchange of meteorological information today.

Unlike data about dangerous weather patterns, cyber data, and the lessons and predictions we can gather from it, are not widely shared. In fact, information hoarding is the norm.

This siloed approach to cyber data may eventually be deadly. That is why over 20 years ago, the U.S. started forming Information Sharing and Analysis Centers (ISACS) to facilitate information sharing for critical infrastructure, like finance, oil and gas and the defense industrial base. ISACS are non-profit organizations that collect, analyze and disseminate actionable cyber threat information among members, providing tools to mitigate risks and enhance resilience.

What We Need to Do

We need to start exporting the weather tracking and reporting model to everything. The goal should be to work towards an international coalition or organization dedicated to sharing cyber intelligence, like the ones we use for weather. But the first step towards that system is for businesses, from engineers to boards, to realize that intel sharing is in their best interest, and in everyone's.

If this is to be viable for companies and public institutions, governments first need to address the fear of retaliation. Regulators should provide enough wiggle room and not be too quick on the trigger when an attack is reported. Some form of safe harbor or legal immunity should be provided. Otherwise, if companies are punished for sharing intel and breach-related data, there is little to no incentive to actually share that data.

Hacker summer camp, the trio of security conferences in Vegas (Black Hat, DEFCON and BSides) just introduced the world to yet another new Microsoft vulnerability, this time leaving unpatched users open to attack. It surely resembles the feeling of coastal cities deep in hurricane season. Companies have been thinking about the second half of 2019 planning, and decisions on 2020 budgets are around the corner. Trust, and its deficit, play a larger role than ever in a company's reputation and success.

A World Economic Forum study makes it clear that customers want secure systems that protect them and their information not only from any current vulnerability but also from any future mutations. The research suggests that 93 percent of executives would pay an average 22 percent more for devices with better security. It's not just about the latest tech. It's about how secure that tech is. Boards that prioritize cybersecurity have an opportunity to differentiate their company and the board itself in the field. Cybersecurity can be a business enabler, but it will only be lip service if not supported by strategic investment in culture, staff and technology.

No system in the world is completely airtight. Connectivity is permeating deeper into our businesses and lives every day. 5G, IoT and cloud adoption have become integral to every competitive business. No matter how much is spent on the latest security tool, being connected to the internet is a risk. If you live on the East Coast, a hurricane eventually will make a landfall near your home. The goal is to prepare—build stronger structures, buy flood insurance, have evacuation plans. But most importantly, to save lives, information that allows you to predict timing and damage needs to be shared.

For cyber incidents that same message holds true. Invest in systems that collect, analyze and warn of threats and organizations that can develop best practices and emergency response plans for when the inevitable does happen. Run regular simulations. Constantly update plans and systems because the threat is always evolving. Most importantly, share the lessons far and wide. Weather doesn't recognize borders; neither do cyberattacks.

Information sharing is everyone's responsibility. Engineers need to report and follow warnings. Above all, boards need to accept and foster a cybersecurity culture. Customers need to demand security. Governments need to be more open. Every single one of us needs to care. If we continue as is, holding information close to our chests, the first death by cyber incident will happen. It's only a matter of time. The international community has come together to make the world safer in the past. We can do it again.

About the Authors

Algirde Pipikaite is project lead at the Center for Cybersecurity, World Economic Forum.

Haiyan Song is senior vice president and general manager, security markets, at Splunk.

Section 3: Big Data In the Wrong Hands

3.1   Blockchain Enhances Privacy, Security and Conveyance of Data
        By Mihaela Ulieru

3.2   Data Thieves Find Easy Pickings in the Health Care System
        By Adam Tanner

3.3   Data Vu: Why Breaches Involve the Same Stories Again and Again
        By Daniel J. Solove, Woodrow Hartzog

3.4   Giant U.S. Computer Security Breach Exploited Very Common Software
        By Sophie Bushwick

3.5   The Equifax Hack—Bad for Them, Worse for Us
        By Paul Rosenzweig

Blockchain Enhances Privacy, Security and Conveyance of Data

By Mihaela Ulieru

Blockchain, the technology behind the bitcoin digital currency, is a decentralized public ledger of transactions that no one person or company owns or controls. Instead, every user can access the entire blockchain, and every transfer of funds from one account to another is recorded in a secure and verifiable form by using mathematical techniques borrowed from cryptography. With copies of the blockchain scattered all over the planet, it is considered to be effectively tamper-proof.

The challenges that bitcoin poses to law enforcement and international currency controls have been widely discussed. But the blockchain ledger has uses far beyond simple monetary transactions.

Like the Internet, the blockchain is an open, global infrastructure upon which other technologies and applications can be built. And like the Internet, it allows people to bypass traditional intermediaries in their dealings with each other, thereby lowering or even eliminating transaction costs.

By using the blockchain, individuals can exchange money or purchase insurance securely without a bank account, even across national borders—a feature that could be transformative for the two billion people in the world currently underserved by financial institutions. Blockchain technology lets strangers record simple, enforceable contracts without a lawyer. It makes it possible to sell real estate, event tickets, stocks and almost any other kind of property or right without a broker.

The long-term consequences for professional intermediaries, such as banks, attorneys and brokers, could be profound—and not necessarily in negative ways, because these industries themselves

60

pay huge amounts of transaction fees as a cost of doing business. Analysts at Santander InnoVentures, for example, have estimated that by 2022, blockchain technology could save banks more $20 billion annually in costs.

Some 50 big-name banks have announced blockchain initiatives. Investors have poured more than $1 billion in the past year into start-ups formed to exploit the blockchain for a wide range of businesses. Tech giants such as Microsoft, IBM and Google all have blockchain projects underway. Many of these companies are attracted by the potential to use the blockchain to address the privacy and security problems that continue to plague Internet commerce.

Because blockchain transactions are recorded using public and private keys—long strings of characters that are unreadable by humans—people can choose to remain anonymous while enabling third parties to verify that they shook, digitally, on an agreement. And not just people: an institution can use the blockchain to store public records and binding promises. Researchers at the University of Cambridge in the U.K., for example, have shown how drug companies could be required to add detailed descriptions of their upcoming clinical drug trials to the blockchain. This would prevent the companies from later moving the goalposts if the trial did not pan out as anticipated, an all-too-common tactic. In London, mayoral candidate George Galloway has proposed putting the city's annual budget on the blockchain ledger to foster collective auditing by citizens.

Perhaps the most encouraging benefit of blockchain technology is the incentive it creates for participants to work honestly where rules apply equally to all. Bitcoin did lead to some famous abuses in trading of contraband, and some nefarious applications of blockchain technology are probably inevitable. The technology doesn't make theft impossible, just harder. But as an infrastructure that improves society's public records repository and reinforces representative and participatory legal and governance systems, blockchain technology has the potential to enhance privacy, security and freedom of conveyance of data—which surely ranks up there with life, liberty and the pursuit of happiness.

About the Author

Mihaela Ulieru is a Research Professor at Carleton University.

Data Thieves Find Easy Pickings in the Health Care System

By Adam Tanner

When the hacker telephoned one of the U.K.'s largest cosmetic surgery chains, his Slavic accent was so thick that the operator struggled to make out what he was saying. Eventually staff at the London-based Harley Medical Group realized the man had stolen the names of 350,000 past and potential clients, and information about the procedures they sought. It was not the crime of the century but the extortionist knew who wanted a breast enhancement, a nose job or a tummy tuck, and he demanded cash—six figures—to keep quiet.

Harley did not pay, according to CEO James Farquharson. Yet the 2014 incident resulted in an eye-catching front-page headline in *The Sun* tabloid and the formerly profitable chain saw the bottom line turn into a loss the following year—even though the hacker never leaked the data. "It knocked us really, really hard," Farquharson says. "It took us about 12 months before we really started to turn the corner."

Some institutions do submit to blackmail. In February the Hollywood Presbyterian Medical Center announced that it paid $17,000 for a de-encryption key after a hacker locked hospital files. Experts say the case was unusual only in the public admission. "It happens all the time, but everyone involved in it wants to keep it low-profile," says Dean Sysman, co-founder of Cymmetria, an Israeli cybersecurity start-up. "In the health care sector, losing all the data is not only something that is a business risk, it is a human life risk."

As hackers probe cyberspace they are finding weaknesses among the vast patchwork of doctors, hospitals and insurers that make up our health care system—many of them unprepared to counter a sophisticated hacker. Heath data thieves typically seek to extort money, obtain medications, get free health care or steal identities for credit cards and tax refunds. A glut of stolen credit cards and resulting lower prices for them on the black market have made medical data especially attractive, says Angel Grant, director of fraud and risk intelligence at RSA Security: "They are looking for new ways to make money, and they see the health care industry as a soft target because they lack the security maturity of other industries." Health care is so ripe for hacking that the sector accounts for more than a third of all of 2016's breaches involving the release of a name and sensitive information, according to a July 19 report by the Identify Theft Resource Center. It lists 538 breaches across all industries affecting nearly 13 million people.

Online, the shadowy Dark Web openly offers stolen health data for sale. "You can use these profiles for Normal Fraud stuff and/or get a brand new health care plan for yourself and with all the advantages that comes with," said one advertisement RSA investigators found. Since 2009 more than 170 million health records in the U.S. have been exposed in data breaches, according to a tally of incidents involving more than 500 records kept by U.S. Department of Health and Human Services. New breaches regularly appear on the site, which lists the name of the institution, the number of people affected and the type of breach—such as theft, hacking or unauthorized access. In recent weeks a heart clinic in Maryland, a dental practice in Ohio, a chiropractic center in Minnesota and a Massachusetts hospital were among those reporting breaches.

Anthem, the second-largest U.S. insurer, said in 2015 that outsiders had stolen personal and employment data and Social Security numbers—but not medical information—on some 78.8 million people in its Blue Cross Blue Shield plans. Massachusetts doctor Gary Lasneski was among the millions whose data was stolen. Not long after he learned of the breach the Internal Revenue Service wrote him saying they suspected a fraudster had filed a tax return in his name. Initially, he shrugged off the news. "Because I pay every year, I thought, 'Good, let them file and pay for me,'" he says.

But he soon learned the matter was no joke, because criminals file returns hoping to receive tax refunds. Soon someone tried to set up fraudulent accounts at Best Buy, Office Depot and Capitol

One using Lasneski's information. He later joined a class action lawsuit against Anthem. Health care data breaches cost companies an estimated $2.2 million per incident, leading to collective annual losses of $6.2 billion, according to a study released in May by the Ponemon Institute. Yet many patients stay with their providers even after a breach, because changing doctors, hospitals or insurers is more far complicated than just shopping at a different chain store. By contrast, after Target was breached in 2013 it reported that expenses resulting from the breach in 2013 and 2014 totaled more than a quarter of a billion dollars. Even non-Anthem clients had data stolen in the same breach—which I had learned when I received a breach notification letter that Anthem later disclosed after my inquiries was because they were administering a drug plan for CVS Caremark, which partnered with my previous insurer.

Whether a single-doctor office or medical insurance company, health providers must make it more difficult for hackers to penetrate their systems, experts agree. The same applies to companies paid to process their information. Yet consumers need to pay more attention as well by taking measures such as monitoring their electronic health records. "Most portals will send an alert to you to let you know there was a modification to your record," RSA's Grant says. "Just by seeing that and knowing that you haven't ordered something, that you haven't gone to the doctor, that should be a red flag."

Some health care organizations are beefing up security but most continue to lag in sectors such as finance and banking, experts say, noting that many are simply not investing enough time and energy to address the issue. "The majority of both health care organizations and BAs [business associates] have not invested in the technologies necessary to mitigate a data breach nor have they hired enough skilled IT security practitioners," concluded Ponemon's latest annual survey on the subject.

Harley Medical's Farquharson agrees with this assessment and admits his firm's old Web site was vulnerable. Others would prefer not to concede such shortcomings publicly. Three other CEOs hit by medical breaches in recent years—including Anthem head Joseph Swedish—declined interview requests for this article.

About the Author

Adam Tanner is author of Our Bodies, Our Data: How Companies Make Billions Selling Our Medical Records.

Data Vu: Why Breaches Involve the Same Stories Again and Again

By Daniel J. Solove, Woodrow Hartzog

I n the classic comedy *Groundhog Day*, protagonist Phil, played by Bill Murray, asks "What would you do if you were stuck in one place and every day was exactly the same, and nothing that you did mattered?" In this movie, Phil is stuck reliving the same day over and over, where the events repeat in a continual loop, and nothing he does can stop them. Phil's predicament sounds a lot like our cruel cycle with data breaches.

Every year, organizations suffer more data spills and attacks, with personal information being exposed and abused at alarming rates. While Phil eventually figured out how to break the loop, we're still stuck: the same types of data breaches keep occurring with the same plot elements virtually unchanged.

Like Phil eventually managed to do, we must examine the recurring elements that allow data breaches to happen and try to learn from them. Common plotlines include human error, unnecessary data collection, consolidated storage and careless mistakes. Countless stories involve organizations that spent a ton of money on security and still ended up breached. Only when we learn from these recurring stories can we make headway in stopping the cycle.

The main plotline of so many data breach stories is human error. Over and over, people fall for phishing scams, fail to patch vulnerable software promptly, lose devices containing vital data, misconfigure servers or slip up in any number of other ways.

Hackers know that humans are the weak link. Many break-ins to company databases occur less by technological wizardry and more by con artistry. For instance, hackers can trick an organization's employees by sending an e-mail that looks like it's coming from one of their supervisors. Doing so is easy: anyone can readily learn the names of supervisors by looking them up on LinkedIn and can then spoof an e-mail address. Essentially, hackers hack humans more than they do machines.

Despite the fact that human error is an aspect of most data breaches, many organizations have failed to train employees about data security. As for the organizations that do, they often use long and boring training modules that people quickly forget. Not enough attention is paid to making training effective.

It's reasonable to expect that even with a well-trained workforce, some people will inevitably fall for hacker tricks. We must approach data security with realism that people can be gullible and careless, and human nature isn't going to change. That means we need systems and rules in place that anticipate inevitable breaches and minimize their harm.

In many data breaches, an enormous amount of information is lost all at once. because hacked organizations were collecting more data than absolutely necessary, or keeping such information when they should have been deleting it.

Over time, organizations have been collecting and using data faster than they have been able to keep it secure—much like in the 19th-century industrial revolution when factories sprouted up before safety and pollution controls were introduced. Instead of hoarding as much information as possible, they should enact policies of data minimization to collect only data necessary for legitimate purposes and to avoid retaining unnecessary data.

To make matters worse, many organizations have stored the vast troves of information they amass in a single repository. When hackers break in, they can quickly access all the data all at once. As a result, breaches have grown bigger and bigger.

Although many organizations fear a diabolical hacker who can break into anything, what they should fear most are small, careless errors that are continually being made.

For instance, an entirely predictable mistake is a lost device. Lost or stolen laptops, phones and hard drives, loaded up with personal data, have played a big role in breaches. Companies should assume that at least some losses or thefts of portable devices will occur—and to prevent disaster, they should require that the data on them be encrypted. Far too often, there is no planning for inevitable careless mistakes other than hoping that they somehow won't happen.

Money alone is not enough to stop hackers. In fact, many of the organizations that have had big data breaches were also big spenders on data security. They had large security teams on staff. They had tons of resources. And yet, their defenses still were breached. The lesson here is that money must be spent on measures that actually work.

In the case of the Target breach in 2013, the company had spent a fortune on a large cybersecurity team and on sophisticated software to detect unusual activity. This software worked and sent out alerts—but security staff members were not paying enough attention, and reportedly they had turned off the software's automatic defenses. Having the best tools and many people isn't enough. A security team must also have a good playbook, and everyone must do their part.

Although at the surface, data breaches look like a bunch of isolated incidents, they are actually symptoms of deeper, interconnected problems involving the whole data ecosystem. Solving them will require companies to invest in security measures that can ward off breaches long before they happen—which may take new legislation.

With a few exceptions, current laws about data security do not look too far beyond the blast radius of the most recent breach—and that worsens the damage that these cyberattacks cause. Only so much marginal benefit can be had by charging increasing fines to breached entities. Instead, the law should target a broader set of risky actors, such as producers of insecure software and ad networks that facilitate the distribution of malware. Organizations that have breaches almost always could have done better, but there's only so much marginal benefit from beating them up. Laws could focus on holding other actors more accountable, so responsibility is more aptly distributed.

In addition to targeting a wider range of responsible entities, legislation could require data minimization. With reduced data, breaches become much less harmful. Limiting data access to those who need it and can prove their identity is also highly effective. Another underappreciated important protection is data mapping: knowing what data are being collected and maintained, the purposes for having the data, the whereabouts of the data and other key information.

Government organizations could act proactively to hold companies accountable for bad practices before a breach occurs, rather than waiting for an attack. This strategy would strengthen data security more than the current approach of focusing almost entirely on breached organizations.

But the law keeps on serving up the same tired consequences for breached companies instead of trying to reform the larger data ecosystem. As with Phil, until lawmakers realize the errors of their ways, we will be fated to relive the same breaches over and over again.

This is an opinion and analysis article, and the views expressed by the author or authors are not necessarily those of Scientific American.

About the Author

Daniel J. Solove is John Marshall Harlan Research Professor of Law at George Washington University Law School. He is the founder of TeachPrivacy, a company that provides computer-based privacy and data security training. He is co-author of Breached! Why Data Security Law Fails and How to Improve It *(Oxford University Press, 2022).*

Giant U.S. Computer Security Breach Exploited Very Common Software

By Sophie Bushwick

A hacking campaign has gained access to private information from a number of government and industry organizations, including the U.S. Departments of Treasury, Commerce and Homeland Security. The cyberattacks, which were first reported this past weekend, were carried out by compromising a software platform produced by a vendor called SolarWinds.

"We are aware of a potential vulnerability which, if present, is currently believed to be related to updates which were released between March and June 2020 to our Orion monitoring products," Kevin Thompson, president and CEO of SolarWinds, explained in a prepared statement shared via e-mail. "We believe that this vulnerability is the result of a highly-sophisticated, targeted and manual supply chain attack by a nation state. We are acting in close coordination with FireEye, the Federal Bureau of Investigation, the intelligence community, and other law enforcement to investigate these matters."

Because thousands of clients rely on SolarWinds' products, experts expect more breaches to be revealed in the coming days. *Scientific American* spoke with Ben Buchanan, a professor specializing in cybersecurity and statecraft at Georgetown University's School of Foreign Service, about why so many organizations rely on such third-party software and how its compromise made them vulnerable to cyberattack.

[An edited transcript of the interview follows.]

Q: How did the hackers manage to compromise so many groups?
A: The heart of the issue here is that for big organizations, like government agencies or corporations, their computer networks are incredibly complex. And they oftentimes turn to software to

try to manage these computer networks: understand how the traffic flows, what devices are on their network, how things are configured. SolarWinds is an example of this kind of software that seems to be quite widely used throughout the government and industry. But because it's used to manage these networks, it has a position of privilege where it can see a lot of what goes on. If you compromise SolarWinds, it then becomes possible to compromise the broader computer network.

Q: Is that what happened here?

A: That's right. We're still learning more, but what it seems occurred is that hackers somehow gained the ability to manipulate the code of SolarWinds itself; essentially they put a backdoor into SolarWinds that let them carry out malicious activity. And the customers of SolarWinds downloaded this software update to their systems, not realizing it was in part malicious, at some point [after] March—and once they did this, they essentially gave the hackers an entry point into their network. From there the hackers began doing things like harvesting passwords and other credentials to try to get further access to each of these networks that they [had] compromised with the initial toehold given to them by compromising SolarWinds.

With the passwords that they acquired, they almost certainly used that to get access to more computers and more accounts within the target organizations. It seems their end goal was getting not just passwords, but also files and the like, and then pulling those pieces of information back out in an espionage operation. I think it probably is too soon to say how extensive that espionage was, and it's too soon to say how many of the possible victims actually were breached in this way. SolarWinds says it was fewer than 18,000 organizations—which is not a reassuring number, because it's big. That seems to be the upper end on the reach of the espionage operation.

Q: Thousands of organizations use SolarWinds, but how many more rely on other, similar software?

A: I'm sure *every* large organization relies on something similar to manage a network that's particularly complicated. This kind of enterprise management is just part of running a modern, large organization—and the challenge right now is that these organizations have to trust somebody's software. In this case, one of the companies that they trusted turns out to have been breached. I'm sure SolarWinds is not the only organization that's in this position of trust. And I'm sure any organization that sees itself used by so many high-profile targets is itself a target.

Q: How do investigators figure out who is responsible for attacks like this?

A: Just as police investigate a string of bank robberies by looking for a method of operations, or forensic evidence that links one robbery to the next, you can do the same thing with hacking operations. Investigators—often in the private sector, sometimes in the government—will look across a series of cases to build a pattern of operations for the hackers. And they will cluster different patterns of operations to different groups. And what the reporting indicates, in this case, is that the pattern of activity suggested this was the Russian SVR intelligence service that we've seen carry out very sophisticated hacking operations against the United States and worldwide targets before—never a destructive attack, but always these intricate espionage operations that hit high-value targets.

Q: What do you predict is going to happen next?

A: The next step is definitely going to be a very thorough investigation that is one of the most significant cyber investigations we've seen, just because the scope of this breach is so big. We're talking about potentially hundreds or thousands of organizations—likely hundreds I would say—that could have been compromised in this breach. Once an agency as sophisticated as the SVR gets access to a network, they're very hard to get out. So, remediating this breach is going to be difficult. We're going to start to realize, in the weeks to come, some degree of the information that was taken, some degree of who the victims are. [With] every single one of those, I think it's going to be another blow and raise the level of concern about this operation.

Q: How can the cybersecurity community defend against this type of attack?

A: This is a scenario, because the intrusions were so well done, when it's hard to come up with a list of easy fixes. Because these are sophisticated adversaries, they compromised a system, SolarWinds, that was incredibly widely used and widely trusted. They essentially exploited that trust to carry out their operations, and that is something that's really hard to defend against. This is not the same thing as just fixing a single software vulnerability and applying a patch—it's a lot more difficult to combat this kind of threat.

This sheds some light on just how fierce the competition is between nations in cyberspace. We spend a lot of time talking about things like deterrence, norms and signaling between nations. But my view is that this kind of activity—competition, espionage, well below the threshold of conflict, what I call shaping the international environment to suit one's ends—that's par for the course in cybersecurity. So, while this is certainly a high-water mark, the daily competition that leads to events like this is par for the course. And I think we probably need to spend more time in the policy world thinking about the implications of that. It's pretty clear right now [that] the status quo, both in policy and in technology, does not let us deter this activity, and does not let us technically block this activity.

About the Author

Sophie Bushwick is an associate editor covering technology at Scientific American.

The Equifax Hack—Bad for Them, Worse for Us

By Paul Rosenzweig

143 Million. That's the approximate number of records held by Equifax that got stolen by a hacker. Equifax is one of the "Big 3" credit reporting bureaus, so all of the data that it collects is highly sensitive personal and financial data—your credit card charges, your mortgage loans, etc. And, considering that its worldwide holdings are roughly 800 million records, the loss is astronomical—roughly 20 percent of the entire data set went out the door.

How could it happen? Will Equifax be found at fault? And what can we do to prevent it from happening again? All good questions—none with easy answers.

As to how it happened—Equifax is blaming the software. According to the company there was a flaw in the open-source software known as Apache STRUTS created by the Apache Foundation. Open-source software is, as its name implies, created in an open manner through public collaboration and it's also often offered for free, or for a minimal fee, to users. (By contrast, for example, Apple keeps many of its software details confidential and considers it corporate intellectual property.) STRUTS is used by about 65 percent of Fortune 100 companies, including Lockheed Martin, Citigroup, Vodafone, Virgin Atlantic, Reader's Digest, Office Depot, and Showtime—plus the IRS—so any flaw in STRUTS is a problem.

The problem, for Equifax, is that the flaws in STRUTS are well known and widely reported. The U.S. government put out an alert in 2014. And the Apache Foundation has been pretty proactive in deploying fixes that patch the vulnerability. So even though the software may well be at issue, Equifax will have some questions to answer about why it hadn't done everything it could to patch the flaws.

That doesn't mean, however, that Equifax is going to go out of business. They will suffer substantial economic damage, to be sure. In addition to response costs in fixing the problem now, there will be credit monitoring to pay for, legal fees, and probably some sort of fine. But the biggest damage will be to their reputation. The market here is, however, limited—there are only three large credit reporting agencies. So even the reputational damage may not have a real effect on the bottom line. More to the point, the economics are such that suffering a data breach like this is, today, just a "cost of doing business."

Data holders have not been required to internalize the costs of cyber security. Or, as Prof. Zeynep Tufekci put it, we live in a "regulatory environment in which consumers shoulder more and more of the risk, and companies less and less." Naturally, then, we get less security than is societally optimal.

And so, the real loser here is you and me. We have no privacy left. Personally, I have suffered through the Target breach, the Home Depot breach, the OPM (U.S. Office of Personnel Management) breach—where our government lost all the data it had on those who held top-secret clearances—and now the Equifax breaches. Between them I have lost all of my financial, health and identification data, as well as the information that went into my classified background investigation, and the fingerprints off of my hands. There is nothing about me that isn't available somewhere on the network.

For most of us, that's a personal problem with direct effects. My mental health issues, or my financially precarious position, (both hypotheticals by the way) are now an open book. But the bigger issue is systematic and it goes to the integrity of the entire cyber ecosystem. Today, almost all of us prove who we are to others on the network through some form of personal information. "What is your mother's maiden name?" If all of our personal information is now widely available many (all?) of our current methods of authenticating identity are suspect. What is the systematic cost to trust on the network? Think of the contexts (like banking) where trust is essential. How about governmental contexts where orders and directives (some with real world military consequences) can no longer be conclusively verified.

Overly apocalyptic? Perhaps. But a clear sign that we need to rethink identification and authentication. One consequence of the Equifax breach may be mandatory identify verification and the end of anonymity on the network—a truly perverse result.

About the Author

Paul Rosenzweig is founder of Red Branch Consulting PLLC, a homeland security consulting company, and formerly served as Deputy Assistant Secretary for Policy in the Department of Homeland Security.

Section 4: Are Our Elections Vulnerable?

4.1   Are Blockchains the Answer for Secure Elections? Probably Not
       By Jesse Dunietz

4.2   How to Defraud Democracy
       By J. Alex Halderman, Jen Schwartz

4.3   The Vulnerabilities of Our Voting Machines
       By Jen Schwartz

Are Blockchains the Answer for Secure Elections? Probably Not

By Jesse Dunietz

With the U.S. heading into a pivotal midterm election, little progress has been made on ensuring the integrity of voting systems—a concern that retook the spotlight when the 2016 presidential election ushered Donald Trump into the White House amid allegations of foreign interference.

A raft of start-ups has been hawking what they see as a revolutionary solution: repurposing blockchains, best known as the digital transaction ledgers for cryptocurrencies like Bitcoin, to record votes. Backers say these internet-based systems would increase voter access to elections while improving tamper-resistance and public auditability. But experts in both cybersecurity and voting see blockchains as needlessly complicated, and no more secure than other online ballots.

Existing voting systems do leave plenty of room for suspicion: Voter impersonation is theoretically possible (although investigations have repeatedly found negligible rates for this in the U.S.); mail-in votes can be altered or stolen; election officials might count inaccurately; and nearly every electronic voting machine has proved hackable. Not surprisingly, a Gallup poll published prior to the 2016 election found a third of Americans doubted votes would be tallied properly.

Chain Voting

Blockchain advocates say the technology addresses the root cause of voting systems' insecurity—the fact that voting can be controlled by a single person, group or machine. Argentina's "Net Party" provides an example of what can go wrong. The tiny political party fields candidates who promise to strictly follow citizens' bidding as expressed on an online polling platform. When its leaders were pondering interparty alliances in early 2014, they put the decision to a vote among party members. To their horror, they discovered database administrators were selectively delaying new voter registrations until after the referendum, skewing the participant pool toward the administrators' preferred outcome.

Shenanigans like this one are possible only when an official (or a small cabal thereof) can unilaterally decide which votes or voters make the cut. Inspired by this realization, Net Party founder Santiago Siri went on to found Democracy Earth, a blockchain voting start-up. Democracy Earth and its peers aim to prevent corruption by decentralizing the voting process, subjecting each decision and vote to the public review of a blockchain.

Functionally, a blockchain is simply a convoluted database. Each entry in Bitcoin's database, for example, is a transaction in a digital ledger. The ledger publicly lists all transactions to date, implicitly specifying who retains how much money. What distinguishes a blockchain from conventional databases is that it enables multiple parties to share a database without centralized control. Most conventional databases have one authoritative computer that governs the process of adding data. In a blockchain, that trusted gatekeeper is replaced by computers all over the internet, each maintaining its own copy of the database. These computers act as validators for new data: When Alice wants to send money to Bob, she broadcasts the transaction to the validators, which must confirm for themselves the transaction adheres to the blockchain's rules (for example, that Alice has not sent more bitcoins than she owns). Once a majority of the network has accepted the transactions, they become the de facto consensus history.

Although blockchains' most prominent uses are monetary, there is no reason they cannot store other types of data—and votes would seem an excellent fit. An ideal voting system resists corruption by authorities or hackers and empowers citizens and auditors to agree on an election's outcome. Conveniently, auditable consensus among parties who do not fully trust one another is exactly what blockchains offer.

Each of the companies buying into this vision brings its own flavor. One start-up called Votem built its systems around academic research on letting voters check that individual votes were counted. Voatz, another start-up, supplements the blockchain with biometric identity verification, using smartphones' and tablets' built-in fingerprint readers and facial recognition to authenticate voters. Democracy Earth offers the ability to delegate your vote to another voter whose judgment you trust. Smartmatic, a prominent voting technology firm, integrates a blockchain into its broader suite of voting services. Products from these companies and others are attracting tentative interest from U.S. political parties, the U.S. military and governments including those of Brazil and Switzerland.

Details Full of Devils

Still, neither cryptographers nor election experts are impressed with blockchains' potential to improve election integrity. Noted cryptographer Ron Rivest of the Massachusetts Institute of Technology sums up the bleak consensus among academics: "I don't know of any who think it's a good idea, and within one or two years I expect all these companies to die."

Blockchain voting would require more than simply replacing Bitcoin transactions with votes. "Bitcoin works because you don't need [centrally issued] identities," says Arthur Gervais, a blockchain researcher at University College London. Instead, users generate public "addresses," which act like deposit-only account numbers for receiving money, along with secret digital "keys" that are needed to transfer money out of the corresponding accounts. Anyone can create key-address pairs willy-nilly. The catch: there is no recourse if you lose your secret key or leak it to a thief, in which case your address might as well contain the ashes of dollar bills.

This situation will not fly for government elections, where state and local authorities manage lists of eligible voters. Neither would most governments tolerate the possibility of a voter being disenfranchised if their digital voting key is swallowed by a damaged hard drive or stolen by a thief to cast a fraudulent vote.

This is why most blockchain election providers partially centralize the management of voter identities. Their systems are designed to query a consortium of several different identity databases such as government-issued IDs and fingerprints collected during registration to match the voter with a name from government voter rolls. A quorum of these identity authorities can also revoke lost or stolen voting keys. Similarly, the companies partially centralize the validation process to guard against malicious influence: Instead of allowing anyone to become a validator, the government or party organizing the election designates a consortium of universities, nongovernmental organizations and such whose consensus determines what makes it onto the blockchain.

Unlike a Bitcoin-style open model, this consortium-managed blockchain model is at least implementable without damaging the election process, says Joe Kiniry, CEO of elections security company Free & Fair and principal scientist at Galois, a software company specializing in trustworthy software. But switching to a consortium also wipes out the blockchain's supposed security benefits. Having voter identities dispensed and revoked by central authorities puts voters back at the mercy of a few administrators who can decide which votes count. The role of validators, meanwhile, is reduced to auditing for fraudulent votes, which can be achieved far more simply. "Blockchains are a very interesting and useful technology for distributed consensus where there is no central authority. But elections just don't fit that model," says Microsoft senior cryptographer Josh Benaloh. Once a central entity is coordinating an election, "you might as well have that entity publish [vote] data on [a Web site], digitally sign it and be done."

In fact, Kiniry and Gervais both contend blockchain technology does not even solve the core problems of online election integrity. "If you look at all the technology components necessary," Kiniry says, a blockchain "only ticks, like, the first four boxes out of a hundred." It works for recording votes, but even blockchain start-ups need additional layers of technology for thornier challenges such as validating voters, keeping ballots secret and letting each voter verify their vote was tallied.

Cryptographers have spent decades advocating for their preferred solutions to those challenges—a suite of techniques known as "end-to-end verifiable voting." These techniques make no use of blockchains; in fact, Benaloh says they solve all the problems a blockchain does and then some. Ironically, though, helping end-to-end verifiability go mainstream might end up being blockchains' greatest contribution to election security. After all, the word "blockchain" draws investor cash even to companies whose connection to the technology is, speaking generously, tenuous. And even skeptics acknowledge blockchains' relevance to voting; despite their questionable utility for security, similar procedures can enhance voting systems' efficiency or reliability. So someone may well find a way to build a cryptographer-approved system and call it a blockchain. What if that's what it takes for end-to-end verifiability to get traction? "If that's what makes you adopt it, okay, let's do it," Benaloh says. "But I want to talk about all the real benefits of a good protocol as well."

About the Author

Jesse Dunietz is a computer scientist and the Technology, Energy, and Society Fellow at Securing America's Future Energy (SAFE).

How to Defraud Democracy

By J. Alex Halderman, Jen Schwartz

J. *Alex Halderman is a computer scientist who has shown just how easy it is to hack an election. His research group at the University of Michigan examines how attackers can target weaknesses in voting machinery, infrastructure, polling places and registration rolls, among other features. These days he spends much of his time educating lawmakers, cybersecurity experts and the public on how to better secure their elections. In the U.S., there are still serious vulnerabilities heading into the 2020 presidential contest.*

Given the cracks in the system, existing technological capabilities and the motivations of adversaries, Halderman has speculated here on potential cybersecurity disasters that could throw the 2020 election—and democracy itself—into question. Halderman, however, is adamant about one thing: "The only way you can reach certainty that your vote won't be counted is by not casting it. I do not want to scare people off from the polls." What follows is based on two conversations that took place in October 2018 and June 2019; it has been edited and condensed.

The 2016 U.S. presidential election really did change everything. It caught much of the intelligence and cybersecurity communities off guard and taught us that our threat models for cyberwarfare were wrong. Thanks to the Mueller report, we now know that the Russians made a serious and coordinated effort to undermine the legitimacy of the 2016 election outcome. Their efforts were, I think, far more organized and multipronged than anyone initially realized. And to my knowledge, no state has since done any kind of rigorous forensics on their voting machines to see if they had been compromised. I am quite confident that the Russians will be back in 2020.

I think the intelligence community will continue to try to gain visibility into what malicious actors are planning and what they're doing. It's incredible, really, how much detail has come out of the indictments about specific actions by specific people in the Russian military and leadership. But it's hard to know what we're not seeing. And do we have a parallel level of visibility into North Korea or Iran or China? There are potentially a lot of sophisticated nation- state actors that would want to do us harm in 2020 and beyond.

Since the 2016 elections many states have made improvements to their election machinery, but it's not enough, nor is it happening quickly enough. There are still 40 states that are using voting machines that are at least a decade old, and many of these machines are not receiving software patches for vulnerabilities. Nearly 25 percent of states do not have complete paper trails, so they cannot do postelection auditing of physical ballots. Election security is not a partisan issue. Yet there are roadblocks, especially oming from Republican leadership in the Senate, that make it unlikely that an election security bill is going to advance. I think that is a terrible abdication of Congress's duty to provide for the common defense. Thus, many of the worst-case scenarios for election interference are still going to be possible in 2020.

Leading Up to Election Day

Cyberwarfare often involves exploiting known vulnerabilities in systems and the basic limits of people's psychology and gullibility. During the primaries and in the months leading up to the election, influence operations on social media are going to get much more precise and data-driven than ever before—and therefore more effective and harder to detect.

Already presidential candidates are finely crafting political advertisements to specific demographics of voters to maximally influence them. So, you might receive one message from a candidate based on what's known about you in consumer databases. And people with slightly different views on certain issues might receive a different message from the same candidate. Of course, the bad guys who are trying to spread outright fictions will begin to harness the same strategy.

As we saw in 2016, one of the goals of attackers is to increase the amount of divisiveness in society—to reduce social cohesion. Suppose the Russians purchase access to the same consumer-profile data that advertisers in political campaigns use to target you. They can combine that with data from political polls and purchased (or stolen) voter-registration lists to figure out exactly how much your individual vote matters and use those tools to push customized disinformation at narrow groups of people. Attackers may even impersonate political candidates. In a crowded Democratic primary season, there will be sweeping opportunity to deploy microtargeted messaging to turn people against one another, even when they agree about most things.

We all assume that more transparency is a good thing. But people have always taken facts out of context when it is helpful to them and harmful to their opponents. Candidates increasingly live with the threat of targeted theft of true information. When information is selectively stolen from particular groups that an attacker wants to disadvantage, the truth can be used as a powerful and one-sided political weapon—and as we saw with the 2016 Hillary Clinton campaign, it was incredibly effective. It is such a fundamental threat to our notions of how the truth in journalism should play out in a democratic process that I'm sure it's going to happen again. And it can get a lot worse than the theft of e-mails. Imagine someone hacking into candidates' smartphones and secretly recording them during private moments or while talking to their aides. My research group is polling political campaigns to assess how well they are protecting themselves from this, and so far I don't think they are ready.

We're also going to see information that is doctored or entirely synthetic and made to appear real. In some ways, this creates a worse threat. Attackers don't have to actually catch the candidate saying something or e-mailing something if they can produce a record that is indistinguishable from the truth. We've seen recent advances in using machine learning to synthesize video of people saying things that they never actually said on camera. Overall, these tactics help to undermine our basic notions of what's true and what's not. It makes it easier for candidates to deny real things that they said by suggesting that the content of e-mails and recordings were forged and that people shouldn't be believing their own eyes and ears. It's a net loss for our ability to form political consensus based on reality.

Meanwhile each state runs its own independent voter-registration system. Since 2016 many states have taken great strides to protect those systems by installing better network-intrusion detection systems or by upgrading antiquated hardware and software. But many have not.

During the last election, Russians probed or attempted to get into voter-registration systems in at least 18 states. Some sources quote higher numbers. And according to the Senate Select Committee on Intelligence's findings, in some of those states the Russians were in a position to alter or destroy the registration data. If they follow through this time, across entire states people will go to the polls and be told that they aren't on the lists. Maybe they will be given provisional ballots. But if this happens to a large fraction of voters, then there will be such terrible delays that many will give up and go home. A sophisticated attacker could even cause the registration system to lie to voters who confirm their own registration status through online portals while corrupting information in the rolls that are used in polling places.

Attacks on preelection functions could be engineered to have a racial or partisan effect. Because of antidiscrimination laws, some voter-registration records include not only political affiliation but also race. With access to that database, someone could easily manipulate only the records belonging to people of a certain political party, racial group or geographical location.

In some states, online voter-registration systems also allow the voter to request an absentee ballot or to change the address to which the ballot is directed. An attacker could request vote-by-mail ballots for a large number of citizens and direct them to people working with the attacker who would fill them in and cast fake votes.

On Election Day

Election interference can be successful in many ways—it depends on an attacker's goals and level of access. In a close election, if a coordinated group, say in Russia, thinks one candidate is much better than the other for their country, why not try to influence the outcome by undetectably manipulating votes? An attacker could infiltrate what are called election-management systems. There is a programming process by which the design of the ballot—the races and candidates and the rules for counting the votes—gets produced and then gets copied to every individual voting machine. Election officials usually copy it on memory cards or USB sticks for the election machines. That provides a route by which malicious code could spread from the centralized programming system to many voting machines in the field. Then the attack code runs on the individual voting machines, and it's just another piece of software. It has access to all the same data that the voting machine does, including all the electronic records of people's votes.

For 2020 I think ground zero for this kind of vote manipulation via cyberattack is an office building in the Midwest. Much of the country outsources its ballot design to just a few election vendors— the largest of which is a voting-machine manufacturer that, when I visited, told me it does the preelection programming for about 2,000 jurisdictions across 34 states. All of that's done from its headquarters, in a room I've been in that I'd describe as being part of a typical work building shared with other companies. If attackers can hack into that central facility and remotely infiltrate the company's computers, they can spread malicious code to voting machines and change election results across much of the country. The tactic might be as subtle as manipulating vote totals in close jurisdictions. It could easily go undetected.

The scientific consensus is that the best way to secure the vote is to use paper ballots and rigorously audit them, by having people inspect a random sample. Unfortunately, 12 states still don't have paper across the board. And some states, instead of adopting paper, are now having officials do auditing by looking at a scan of the original ballot on a computer screen. We have new research coming out that shows how you can use a computer algorithm to essentially do "deepfake" ballot scans. We used computer-vision techniques to automatically move the check marks around so that the scan of your ballot filled out in your distinctive handwriting reflects votes different from the ones you recorded on the piece of paper.

It might actually be scarier if attackers don't think one candidate is much better for their purposes than the other. Maybe their motivation is more general: to weaken American democracy. They could introduce malicious code that would make the election equipment essentially destroy itself when it is turned on in November 2020, which will cause massive chaos. Or they could have the equipment appear to work, but at the end of the day officials discover that no votes have been recorded. In the jurisdictions without paper backup, there is no other record of the vote. You would have to run a completely new election. The point of this kind of visible attack is that it undermines faith in the system and shakes people's confidence in the integrity of democracy.

Election Night and Beyond

You need to get people to agree more or less about the truth and the conclusion of the election. But by the time November rolls around, we're all going to be primed to worry about the legitimacy of our process. So much is going to depend on how close the race seems on election night.

The way that results get transferred from your local precinct to the display on CNN or on the *New York Times* Web site is through a very centralized computer system operated by the Associated Press and others. What if an attacker were to hack those computer systems and cause the wrong call to be made on election night? We'd eventually find out about it because states go back and do their own totalization, but it might take days or even a couple of weeks until we discover a widespread error. People who want to believe the election was rigged would see this as confirmation it was rigged indeed.

Only 22 states have a requirement to complete any kind of postelection audit of their paper trail prior to legally certifying the results. And in 20 out of those 22 states, the requirement doesn't always result in a statistically significant level of auditing, because they do not look at a large enough ballot sample to have high confidence in the result, especially when results are close. It's just based on the math and has nothing to do with politics. Only Rhode Island and Colorado require a statistically rigorous process called a risk-limiting audit, although other states are moving in that direction.

If, because of computer hacking, we don't arrive at election results in many states, we enter unknown territory. The closest precedent would be something like the 2000 Bush versus Gore election where the outcome was ultimately decided in the Supreme Court and wasn't known for a month after election day. It would be terrifying, and it might involve running the election again in states that were affected. You really can't replay an election and expect to get the same results, because it's always going to be a different political environment.

Or let's say a candidate challenges a close election result. Under current rules and procedures, that is often the only way that people will ever go back and examine the physical evidence to check whether there was an attack. Right now we don't have the right forensic tools to be able to go back and see what happened where and who might have done what. It's not even clear who would have the jurisdiction to do those kinds of tests, because election officials and law enforcement don't often go hand in hand. You don't want to turn it over to the police to decide who won.

In a real nightmare scenario, attackers could gain enough access to the voting system to tip the election result and cause one candidate to win by fraud. Then they could keep that a secret—but engineer it in such a way that at any time in the future, they could prove they had stolen the election.

Imagine a swing state like Pennsylvania, which raced to replace its vulnerable paperless voting machines by the end of 2019. Despite this, the state still doesn't require risk-limiting audits, which means outcome-changing fraud could go undetected. What if the whole election comes down to Pennsylvania, and an attacker was able to hack into its machines and change the reported results? They could set the manipulation so that if you sorted the names of the polling places alphabetically, the least significant digits of the votes for the winning candidate formed the digits of pi—or something like that. It would be a pattern that wouldn't be noticeable but that could later be pointed in a way that undeniably shows the results were fake.

Say this information comes out after the new administration has been in power for a certain amount of time, and no one can deny that the president is not the legitimate winner. Now we have an unprecedented constitutional crisis. Finally, imagine if the nation-state that carries out this attack doesn't release its information publicly but instead uses it to blackmail the person who becomes president. This is pushing slightly into the realm of science fiction, though not by much.

The reality is that most cyberwarfare is more mundane. It's almost certain we're going to see attempts to sow doubt that are connected to the vulnerabilities in the election system just because it is so easy. You don't have to hack into a single piece of election equipment—all you have to do is suggest that someone might have.

It's hard to have an open conversation about the vulnerabilities in the system without risking contributing to attackers' goal of making people feel less confident in the results. But the fundamental problem is that the American election system is based on convincing the public to trust the integrity of the imperfect machinery and the imperfect people who operate it. Ultimately our best defense is to make elections be based on evidence instead of on faith—and it is entirely doable. There are so many problems in cybersecurity and critical infrastructure where you could offer me billions of dollars and decades to do research, and I'd say, *Maybe we can make this a little bit better*. But election-security challenges can be solved without any major scientific breakthroughs and for only a few hundred million dollars. It's just a matter of political will.

Referenced

Securing the Vote: Protecting American Democracy. National Academies of Sciences, Engineering, and Medicine. National Academies Press, 2018.

About the Authors

J. Alex Halderman is a professor of computer science and engineering at the University of Michigan, where he is also director of the Center for Computer Security and Society. He was a 2019 Andrew Carnegie Fellow for his work in educating lawmakers and the public in how to strengthen election cybersecurity.

Jen Schwartz is a senior editor of features at Scientific American *who covers how people are adapting, or not, to a rapidly changing world.*

The Vulnerabilities of Our Voting Machines

By Jen Schwartz

A few weeks ago computer scientist J. Alex Halderman rolled an electronic voting machine onto a Massachusetts Institute of Technology stage and demonstrated how simple it is to hack an election.

In a mock contest between George Washington and Benedict Arnold three volunteers each voted for Washington. But Halderman, whose research involves testing the security of election systems, had tampered with the ballot programming, infecting the machine's memory card with malicious software. When he printed out the results, the receipt showed Arnold had won, 2 to 1. Without a paper trail of each vote, neither the voters nor a human auditor could check for discrepancies. In real elections, too, about 20 percent of voters nationally still cast electronic ballots only.

As the U.S. midterm elections approach, Halderman, among others, has warned our "outmoded and under-tested" electronic voting systems are increasingly vulnerable to attacks. They can also lead to confusion. Some early voters in Texas have already reported votes they cast for Democratic U.S. Senate challenger Beto O'Rourke were switched on-screen to incumbent Republican Sen. Ted Cruz. There's no evidence of hacking, and the particular machines in question are known to have software bugs, which could account for the errors.

Halderman does not think an attack is to blame. "If it was, the candidate switch wouldn't be visible to either the voter nor election officials," he says. "But what's happening in Texas is another warning sign of aging machines not functioning well, which makes them fertile ground for vote-stealing attacks."

Ultimately—whether scenarios like the one in Texas stem from glitchy software, defective machinery or an adversarial hack—one outcome is a loss of confidence in our election process. And as cybersecurity journalist Kim Zetter recently wrote in *The New York Times Magazine*, "It's not too grand to say that if there's a failure in the ballot box, then democracy fails."

Halderman, who directs the University of Michigan Center for Computing and Society, recently spoke with *Scientific American* about the different types of technological threats to democracy—and how good old-fashioned paper can safeguard elections.

[An edited transcript of the interview follows.]

Q: It seems like election interference is occurring all around us, in so many different ways. How is the hacking of voting-machine software related to the disinformation campaigns that show up in our Facebook feeds?

A: Technology is transforming democracy on a lot of different levels, and they're not entirely connected. But they all create vulnerabilities in the way that society forms political opinions, expresses those opinions and translates them into election results.

One form of Russian meddling in the 2016 election, for example, was social media campaigns, which affect political discourse at the level of opinions formed by individuals. But the second prong—the hacking into campaigns, like John Podesta's e-mail—was just so sinister in the way it was picking only on one side. That gets to the very roots of how open societies traditionally rely on information gathering and the media in order to make sound political decisions.

And then there's the third form of hacking: going after the machinery of elections, the infrastructure, polling places, voter registration systems, etcetera. That's where most of my work has been.

Q: How did you end up investigating voting security?

A: It was literally dropped into my lap while I was in grad school at Princeton in 2006. No research group had ever had access to a U.S. voting machine in order to do a security analysis, and an anonymous group offered to give us one to study. Back then

94

there was quite a dispute between researchers who hypothesized there would be vulnerabilities in polling place equipment and the manufacturers that insisted everything was fine.

Q: Over the past decade, how has the field of election cybersecurity changed?

A: It has moved away from a position of hubris. Now that there have been major academic studies there is scientific consensus that here will be vulnerabilities in polling place equipment.

Sometimes the risks or probable failure modes of new technology are totally foreseeable. And that was certainly the case in voting. As paperless computer voting machines were being introduced, there were many computer scientists who—before anyone had even studied one of these machines directly—were saying, "This just isn't a good idea to have elections be conducted by, essentially, black box technology."

On the other hand, the ways in which these failures will be exploited—and the implications of that exploitation—are sometimes a bit harder to foresee. When we did the first voting machine study 10 years ago, we talked about a range of different possible attackers, dishonest election officials and corrupt candidates. But the notion that it would be a foreign government cyber attack, that that would be one of the biggest problems to worry about—well, that was pretty far down on the list. Over the past 10 years cyber warfare went from something that seemed like science fiction to something you read about every almost every day in the newspaper.

2016 really did change everything. It taught us that our threat models were wrong. I think it caught much of the intelligence community off guard, and it caught much of the cybersecurity community off guard. It was surreal to see Russia get so close to actually exploiting the vulnerabilities to harm us.

Q: The Department of Homeland Security and intelligence community say there's no evidence that Russian hackers

95

altered votes in the 2016 presidential election. Can you put
"no evidence" in context?

A: We know for sure that in 2016 the Russians didn't do everything that
they are capable of. Most of the evidence—both of Russian attack
and of Russian restraint—is in the context of voter-registration
systems, which are another back-end system operated by each state.

If you read carefully the statements of the intelligence
communities, our evidence that no votes were changed is that
we apparently didn't hear particular Russian operatives who were
responsible for *other* parts of the attack planning or attempting a
vote-manipulation attack. But that's not very reassuring, because
we don't know what other attackers might have been attempting,
for which we might not have the same level of intelligence insight.
It's hard to know what you don't know. There are other adversaries
who certainly benefit from manipulating American elections,
including other countries like China or North Korea.

The voting machines themselves have received much, much,
much less scrutiny post-2016 from intelligence and defensive
sides—as far as we know in the public sphere anyway. To my
knowledge, no state has done any kind of rigorous forensics on
their voting machines to see whether they had been compromised.

**Q: So potentially there's more going on that's not being looked
at as closely?**

A: That's right. But what we do know from the Senate Intelligence
Committee's report, based on its investigation of the Russian
election interference, was that Russia was in a position to do
more damage than they did to the registration systems. They were
in a position to modify or destroy data in at least some states'
registration systems, which if it had gone undetected, would have
caused massive chaos on Election Day. But they decided not to
pull the trigger.

**Q: When it comes to voting machines themselves, though, how
might malicious code get introduced?**

A: One possibility is that attackers could infiltrate what are called election-management systems. These are small networks of computers operated by the state or the county government or sometimes an outside vendor where the ballot design is prepared.

There's a programming process by which the design of the ballot—the races and candidates, and the rules for counting the votes—gets produced, and then gets copied to every individual voting machine. Election officials usually copy it on memory cards or USB sticks for the election machines. That provides a route by which malicious code could spread from the centralized programming system to many voting machines in the field. Then the attack code runs on the individual voting machines, and it's just another piece of software. It has access to all of the same data that the voting machine does, including all of the electronic records of people's votes.

So how do you infiltrate the company or state agency that programs the ballot design? You can infiltrate their computers, which are connected to the internet. Then you can spread malicious code to voting machines over a very large area. It creates a tremendously concentrated target for attack.

Q: Where does this leave us heading into the midterms?

A: Although there's greatly increased security awareness (and increased protection for registration systems in particular) compared to 2016, there are so many gaps left in election security—particularly when it comes to polling place equipment. It would certainly be possible to sabotage election systems in ways that would cause massive chaos. If nothing happens this November, it's going to be because our adversaries chose not to pull the trigger. Not because they had no way of doing us harm.

Q: What if an adversary's goal isn't widespread chaos, but something subtler?

A: Unfortunately, it's also possible to more subtly manipulate things, especially in close elections, in ways that would result in the wrong candidates winning—and with high probability of that not being detected.

Q: I'm thinking about close races for the Senate and the House, such as in Texas and in Georgia.

A: The broader question is if we're going to have a tight national contest for control of Congress, it's going to hinge on a set of swing districts. Because our election system is so distributed, with localities and states making their own critical security decisions, it means some are going to be much weaker than others. And sophisticated adversaries like Russia could try to probe the election security across all of those likely swing districts, find the ones that are most weakly protected and subtly manipulate results in those districts. And if they can do it in enough swing districts, they can flip the outcome—and control of Congress. That's what's so scary.

Q: The National Academies of Sciences, Engineering and Medicine released a report in September that urged all states to adopt paper ballots before 2020. Why is paper best for verifying election outcomes?

A: The idea of a post-election paper audit is a form of quality control. You want to have people inspect enough of the paper records to confirm with high statistical probability that the outcome on the paper and the outcome on the electronic results is the same. You're basically doing a random sample. How large a sample you need depends on how close the election result was. If it was a landslide, a very small sample—maybe even just a few hundred random ballots selected from across the state—could be enough to confirm with high statistical confidence that it was indeed a landslide. But if the election result was a tie, well, you need to inspect every ballot to confirm that it was a tie.

The key insight behind auditing as a cyber defense is that if you have a paper record that the voter got to inspect, then that can't later be changed by a cyber attack. The cost to do so is relatively low. My estimate is it would cost about $25 million a year to audit to high confidence every federal race nationally.

But this strategy is a problem for states like New Jersey and Georgia, where currently there's no paper trail at all.

Today only about 79 percent of votes across the country are recorded on a piece of paper. If you have no paper trail, then it's impossible to perform a rigorous audit. At best you're just hitting the print button again on a computer program. You're going to get the same result you got the first time, whether it is true or not.

There are about 14 specific states that have gaps where ballots aren't being recorded on paper, and that's known to everyone. Georgia, for example, is entirely paperless. And they are also using voting machines with software that hasn't [had a security patch] since 2005.

Q: What are you most concerned about in the 2018 midterm elections?

A: That it's too late to do anything else. Except for maybe some states to tighten up their postelection procedures.

The focus needs to start being on 2020. Because it's going to take that long for some states to replace their aging and vulnerable voting machines, and to make sure that every state has rigorous postelection audits in place. We have an opportunity to solve this problem. It's one of the few grand cybersecurity challenges that doesn't have to be difficult or expensive.

But it's going to take national leadership and national standards to get there. Otherwise we're not going to be able to move fast enough or in a coordinated manner, and the attackers that have us in their sights are going to win.

About the Author

Jen Schwartz is a senior editor of features at Scientific American *who covers how people are adapting, or not, to a rapidly changing world.*

Section 5: White Hats vs. Black Hats

5.1   CSI: Cyber-Attack Scene Investigation: A Malware Whodunit
       By Larry Greenemeier

5.2   FBI Takes Down Hive Criminal Ransomware Group
       By Sophie Bushwick

5.3   Hacking the Ransomware Problem
       By The Editors of *Scientific American*

5.4   The Imperfect Crime: How the WannaCry Hackers Could
       Get Nabbed
       By Jesse Dunietz

5.5   Women in Cybersecurity: Where We Are and Where We're Going
       By Nahal Shahidzadeh

CSI: Cyber-Attack Scene Investigation: a Malware Whodunit

By Larry Greenemeier

C yber attacks against government agencies, infrastructure providers and other high-profile targets are regularly in the news, stirring talk of digital warfare and international sanctions. The forensic investigations that follow these hacks can reveal the method and magnitude of an attack. Pinpointing the culprit, however, is frustratingly more difficult, resulting in little more than vague accusations that the guilty parties (might be) working for a particular foreign government or cyber gang.

Case in point: the recent cyber attacks that shut off power to 80,000 Ukrainians and infiltrated computers at the country's largest airport. Some Ukrainian officials were quick to point the finger at the Kremlin due to their ongoing conflict and because the attacks apparently came from computers in Russia. Others, however, caution Internet addresses can be spoofed and that, even though investigators have recovered some of the "BlackEnergy" malicious software (malware) at fault, they are unable to figure out exactly who wrote it.

Circumstantial Evidence

"Attribution is a curious beast," says Morgan Marquis-Boire, a senior researcher at the University of Toronto's Citizen Lab and former member of Google's security team. "There are a variety of techniques that you can use to make educated assertions about the nature of an attack." These include examining the sophistication of the tools involved, the techniques, the type of data stolen and where it was sent. "I call this strong circumstantial, and this is how a lot of the attribution is done in public malware reports."

Stronger attribution is possible but requires the right type of data. In a few cases that information has come from the trove of documents leaked in 2013 by Edward Snowden, the self-exiled, former U.S. National Security Agency (NSA) contractor. One set of documents informed European Union officials that the NSA had tapped E.U. computer networks. Some of the documents also revealed that a British surveillance agency—Government Communications Headquarters (GCHQ)—was spying on Belgacom, Belgium's largest communications provider, which is partly state-owned. In both cases cyber investigators later identified Regin, a complex piece of malware, as the spyware used to steal secret information out of the targeted networks. Neither U.S. nor British intelligence have claimed authorship of Regin, however, so even with Snowden's help most researchers will not go out on a limb to say with complete confidence that the NSA spied on E.U. officials or that GCHQ hacked Belacom.

Most of the time highly confidential leaked documents are not available, and investigators must deal head-on with malware specifically written to avoid detection and cover the author's tracks. A cyber attack or data theft investigation is in many ways analogous to the work depicted in *Law & Order, CSI: Crime Scene Investigation* or any other fictional police procedural. Cybersecurity forensic investigators frequently begin by analyzing infected computers (the body) and the malware (murder weapon) that took them down. They can learn a lot from even a portion of a malware program by studying the code used, how it was written and how it communicated back with the person or group who wrote it.

Malware written using a lot of customized code suggests a skilled, well-equipped programmer who is very knowledgeable about the computers and network targeted. The use of more generic or open-source code, on the other hand, might be less effective but it also lacks distinguishing characteristics that might be traced back to a particular programmer or organization. Cyber attackers likewise might go with simpler tools so as not to tip their hand regarding the full extent of their capabilities, Marquis-Boire says.

Digital Fingerprinting

Marquis-Boire and other cybersecurity researchers are developing new ways to build malware profiles that serve as digital fingerprints to identify a particular program's formatting styles, how it allocates memory, the ways it attempts to avoid detection and other attributes. Investigators can also learn a lot by the way a programmer names certain features in a program or the way they configure the malware to transmit purloined data, Marquis-Boire says. Forensic malware examinations alone will not expose who is behind a particular cyber attack but they are a key piece of any investigation, he adds.

In one instance Marquis-Boire and University of Toronto colleague Bill Marczak analyzed e-mails received by Bahraini activists and found a piece of spyware intended to steal information from their computers. Further study of the spyware revealed similarities with the FinFisher surveillance software that Gamma International sells to law enforcement agencies. Gamma has denied selling the software to the Bahraini government for spying on its people and suggested the regime may have used a pirated copy to spy on the activists, along with prominent lawyers and opposition politicians. In typical fashion a government had been caught almost, but not quite, in the act.

Other researchers are applying machine learning to automate the matching of coders with their creations. Although malware is usually a compiled program—as opposed to raw source code—that is altered so it cannot be recognized by antivirus software, investigators can identify various obfuscation techniques and start to see patterns across different pieces of malware, says Aylin Caliskan-Islam, a Princeton University postdoctoral research associate. Caliskan-Islam and her colleagues last year produced a study in which they used algorithms to automate the analysis of coding styles from 1,600 programmers, correctly attributing authorship with 94 percent accuracy. They found that the more skilled a programmer is and the more complex the code they use, the easier it is to connect them with their programs.

One of the biggest challenges in applying this approach to malware outside the lab is the lack of "ground truth" attribution data that can be used to train the machine-learning algorithms. "The more samples we have in the past with known programmers, the more easily we can extract coding styles and train our machine-learning models to identify them," Caliskan-Islam says. One of her goals is to partner with a cybersecurity company that can provide her with data from real-world investigations and use that data to further develop her algorithms.

Close to the Vest

Governments also have access to vast amounts of data that could help with cyber forensic investigations. It is in their best interest, however, not to share what they know out of concerns that they will reveal too much about their cyber-snooping programs. There's a good reason that the U.S. government would not reveal much about why it explicitly blamed North Korea for the 2014 cyber attacks on Sony Pictures Entertainment, according to Marquis-Boire. "I wouldn't expect them to make their evidence public," he says. "The NSA has unprecedented and unparalleled access to the workings of the Internet." If they publicize what they know about certain cyber attacks, the perpetrators might use the information to alter their approach.

That would add yet another advantage that cyber attackers have over the people trying to catch them.

About the Author

Larry Greenemeier is the associate editor of technology for Scientific American, *covering a variety of tech-related topics, including biotech, computers, military tech, nanotech and robots.*

FBI Takes Down Hive Criminal Ransomware Group

By Sophie Bushwick

I n ransomware attacks, hackers encrypt a computer system and then extort victims to pay up or risk losing access to their data. Victims have included large companies such as the meat supplier JBS, major infrastructure such as the Colonial Pipeline and entire countries such as Costa Rica. The Department of Justice recently announced some rare good news about this criminal industry: The FBI infiltrated a major ransomware group called Hive and obtained its decryption keys. These keys let the ransomware victims recover their data without paying the demanded fee. The FBI's work helped affected parties avoid paying $130 million. Afterward American law enforcement worked with international partners to seize Hive's servers and take down its website.

According to the DOJ, Hive has been a major player in the ransomware space since June 2021, attacking more than 1,500 victims in more than 80 countries and extorting more than $100 million from them. "I'd say that's up there with the largest ransomware groups we've got data on, in terms of how many organizations have been impacted and how much money is being paid out," says Josephine Wolff, an associate professor of cybersecurity policy at Tufts University. *Scientific American* spoke with Wolff about how the FBI took down Hive and how much of an impact this law-enforcement operation will have on other ransomware criminals.

[An edited transcript of the interview follows.]

Q: What action did the FBI take against Hive?
A: There are two parts of this, both of which are really interesting. The first thing that law enforcement did was to actually infiltrate their internal communications for a period of several months— we think going back to last summer, based on what the Justice

Department has said. And because law enforcement was inside their computers and able to see who they had infected and, more important, what the decryption keys were to undo that ransomware, the Justice Department has said it was able to help lots of victims who had been targeted and actually unencrypt their systems by essentially stealing those decryption keys from the Hive servers without Hive's knowledge of what was going on. So for months you had an undercover presence in those servers of law enforcement, taking decryption keys and giving them to victims so they can recover their computers.

The second part of that, which is what just happened, is the takedown. And that's where the Justice Department actually goes in and seizes servers and removes Hive's website. For that part, it's harder to know what the long-term impacts will be because servers and websites are replaceable. So it's a good disruption, but it's not necessarily equivalent to saying, "These people will never be able to distribute ransomware again." And my guess would be that the reason the takedown happened is because the law-enforcement presence in Hive's system had been detected. Because otherwise I think you would try to maintain that presence as long as you reasonably could.

Q: Is the FBI likely to continue putting together operations like this that involve embedding agents in the systems of criminal organizations for months?

A: Honestly, I hope so. It's a tricky thing to do because many cybercriminal organizations, for obvious reasons, are fairly cautious about who has access to their servers. My guess is that this is a little bit of an anomaly, finding one that was poorly protected enough. Perhaps that is also tied to the fact that Hive is a "ransomware as a service" organization: you see them renting out their malware to a bunch of other bad actors. Therefore, it is being used quite widely by a whole bunch of different entities in this space, and they have a lot of dealings with people who are not internal, known members of their own organization but are customers buying their services. Perhaps that made it easier to introduce new people to the organization and the systems. Certainly this is something law enforcement will keep trying to do. I hope it'll be successful.

Q: Will Hive's downfall deter other ransomware groups?

A: That depends a little bit on some of the next steps. I think this is not a story that's necessarily going to make cybercriminals run in fear. My guess is that some of the larger organizations are going to be sweeping their own systems and looking for any signs of a similar presence that they should pay attention to. I don't know that it's going to make anybody tone down their ransomware operations, partly because I think there's less attention to that and less fear of that for cybercriminals who operate overseas. But it's certainly going to give people some nervousness about the possibility of their own systems being infiltrated in this manner.

Q: What else have these groups been up to lately? What's the current state of the ransomware world?

A: We continue to see these fairly significant, really impactful ransomware attacks on health-care institutions, at local and national government levels, at private institutions. My sense, certainly from insurers, has been that the rate of ransomware has slowed a bit in the past six months to a year—that it's not as frequent or as common as it was perhaps in 2020, 2021, at the moment when it was doing the most damage and causing the greatest number of claims. But that's not to say it's gone away.

Q: Why is that slowdown happening?

A: There are different ideas about that. Many of the insurers would say, "We've gotten better at requiring policyholders to take certain measures to protect themselves"—the most straightforward of which is creating backups, requiring that everyone be able to reboot their systems if everything gets encrypted. And they think that has helped reduce, at least, the number of claims and the amount of damages caused by ransomware attacks. To some extent, the war in Ukraine throws the ransomware industry into some amount of disarray. There's a set of ransomware groups and cybercrime organizations that have people in Ukraine, often leaders based in Russia, who are starting to leak information about each other and undermine each other's efforts from within.

The other piece of it is pretty aggressive policing in the U.S. but also in Europe: trying to catch people, do takedowns and make ransomware a less lucrative crime. Some of that also centers on regulation of the cryptocurrency industry: trying to sanction certain cryptocurrency exchanges that criminals are using to process these payments. Cryptocurrency intermediaries facilitate currency payments at scale and across national borders, which is so essential for this to be a profitable business. Another thing that the U.S. government definitely is pursuing is the international partnership piece. Most of these criminals are based not in the U.S. or other countries where most of the victims are located. Taking them down requires very active collaboration with law enforcement overseas.

Q: Are cybercriminals changing up their tactics to counter the more robust response from law enforcement?

A: One piece we haven't touched on a lot is the question of what happens when ransomware operators don't just encrypt a victim's system but also steal copies of all their data and then threaten, "If you don't pay a ransom, I'm going to leak all of your data online." And that has been growing in frequency for the past couple of years. It's particularly problematic when you think about solutions we've seen, where the hope is "if we provide the decryption key, then people won't pay the ransom." If there's a stolen copy that's being held over a victim's head, that's a less effective mitigation.

Q: What else can we learn from Hive's takedown?

A: In the Department of Justice announcement, they said that when they were inside the Hive servers, they could see who was being targeted. But they were only getting reports from about 20 percent of those victims. This gives us one data point for what percent of ransomware attacks are actually being directly reported to the FBI versus the ones for which the FBI had to proactively reach out and say, "It looks like this ransomware group may have impacted you. We think we can help." Twenty percent is a pretty low number in terms of trying to understand the scale of this problem beyond what people voluntarily report.

About the Author

Sophie Bushwick is an associate editor covering technology at Scientific American.

Hacking the Ransomware Problem

By The Editors of *Scientific American*

During a ransomware hack, attackers infiltrate a target's computer system and encrypt its data. They then demand a payment before they will release the decryption key to free the system. This type of extortion has existed for decades, but in the 2010s it exploded in popularity, with online gangs holding local governments, infrastructure and even hospitals hostage. Ransomware is a collective problem—and solving it will require collaborative action from companies, the U.S. government and international partners.

In 2020 the Federal Bureau of Investigation received more than 2,400 reports of ransomware attacks, which cost victims at least $29 million, not counting lost time and other resources. The numbers underestimate the total impact of ransomware because not all organizations are willing to report it when they fall victim to this crime—and if they do, they do not always share how much they paid. Even these limited statistics, however, demonstrate the increasing boldness of ransomware gangs: the number of attacks in 2020 increased by 20 percent compared with the previous year, and the amount of money paid out more than tripled.

These attacks harm more than the direct targets. In May 2021, for example, Colonial Pipeline announced that its data had fallen prey to a hacking group. As a result, the private company—which transports about half of the East Coast's fuel supply—had to shut down 5,500 miles of pipeline. When they heard the news, people panicked and began stocking up on gas, causing shortages. The company paid at least $4.4 million to restore its systems, although the government eventually recovered about half that amount from the attackers, a Russia-based ransomware gang called REvil.

As long as victims keep paying, hackers will keep profiting from this type of attack. But cybersecurity experts are divided on whether the government should prohibit the paying of ransoms. Such a ban would disincentivize hackers, but it would also place some organizations in a moral quandary. For, say, a hospital, unlocking the computer systems as quickly as possible could be a matter of life or death for patients, and the fastest option may be to pay up.

Other solutions are more straightforward and involve pushing organizations to protect themselves better. Cybersecurity defenses, such as multifactor-authentication requirements and better training in how to recognize phishing and other attacks, make it harder for hackers to access systems. Segmenting one's network means that breaking through to one part of the system does not make all data immediately available. And regular backups allow a company to function even if its original data are encrypted.

All these measures, however, require resources that not all organizations have access to. Meanwhile ransomware gangs are adopting increasingly sophisticated techniques. Some work for weeks to gain entry to a company's network and then worm their way through the system, finding the most vital data to hold hostage. Some groups, including REvil, deliberately compromise an organization's data backups. Others sell instructions and software to help other hackers launch their own attacks. As a result, security personnel must engage in a constant game of cat and mouse.

Collective action can help. If all organizations that fall victim to ransomware report their attacks, they will contribute to a trove of valuable data, which can be used to strike back against attackers. For example, certain ransomware gangs may use the exact same type of encryption in all their attacks. "White hat" hackers can and do study these trends, which allows them to retrieve and publish the decryption keys for specific types of ransomware. Many companies, however, remain reluctant to admit they have experienced a breach, wishing to avoid potential bad press. Overcoming that reluctance may require legislation, such as a bill introduced in the Senate in 2021 that would require companies to report having paid a ransom within 24 hours of the transaction.

Striking back against ransomware will also involve bringing the fight to the criminals—and that requires international cooperation. Last October the FBI worked with foreign partners to force the REvil ransomware gang offline; in November international law-enforcement agencies arrested alleged affiliates of the group. Such collective action among organizations, government and law enforcement will be necessary to curb the boldest ransomware attacks. But it is an ongoing battle—and there is no end in sight.

The Imperfect Crime: How the WannaCry Hackers Could Get Nabbed

By Jesse Dunietz

W hen hackers unleashed the WannaCry "ransomware" in mid-May, not only did they wreak havoc on European hospitals, telecoms and railways, they also made off with a profit. The malicious software locked up thousands of computers' files and demanded $300 ransom payments in order to decrypt them. Victims have so far ponied up more than $140,000 in bitcoin, the digital currency whose reputation for anonymity attracts the libertarian-leaning, the privacy-minded—and the criminally inclined.

Contrary to its reputation, however, bitcoin is quite traceable, making such large attacks harder to profit from than people initially thought. Even after the WannaCry hackers attempted earlier this month to launder their money into a more anonymous bitcoin alternative called monero, experts say it will take an extraordinarily meticulous effort to cash out without leaving digital bread crumbs.

The WannaCry attack operated by infecting out-of-date Windows computers, encrypting their files and automatically generating a message directing victims to pay a ransom or permanently lose their data (hence the term ransomware). In the days after the attack, however, many speculated the perpetrators had already shot themselves in the foot. Well-designed ransomware instructs each victim to pay into a fresh bitcoin "address," which University of Surrey computer scientist Alan Woodward compares with a Swiss bank account number; the address can receive money and anyone with the keys can spend the money, but the address itself contains no identifying information. That allows addresses storing ransoms to hide innocently among the thousands of new addresses created daily. But the WannaCry software had each victim send the spoils to one of just three different addresses—telling the authorities exactly where to look.

This might not pose a problem for the crooks were it not for the fact that all bitcoin transactions are public. At the heart of the system is the "blockchain"—a giant list of every bitcoin transaction that has ever occurred, with new ones submitted and confirmed by participating computers in a decentralized, elegantly orchestrated protocol. Each blockchain entry describes a transfer of money among addresses—for example, "at 12:01 P.M. on August 9, Address A and Address B gave one bitcoin each to Address C."

Addresses are thus not truly anonymous, but rather function as pseudonyms. If the authorities know ransomers own an address, the blockchain gives them an easy trail to follow to see where the money is flowing. And if law enforcement identifies the owners of any account to which the money is moved or if the ATMs or online cryptocurrency exchanges at which the owners cash out know their identities (as is generally required by law), the game is up for the extortionists.

Mixing and Matching

Less than five years ago—in the early days of bitcoin—criminals felt so assured of the cryptocurrency's anonymity that they built their business models on it, says Michael Gronager, CEO of bitcoin analysis company Chainalysis. But in 2015 two law enforcement agents who had been investigating the bitcoin-based black market Silk Road were prosecuted for a number of crimes, including fraud and money laundering, in part on the basis of blockchain analysis by Chainalysis and others. The takeaway for criminals was clear: get smart about bitcoin anonymity or get caught.

One option was to launder ill-gotten gains by "mixing" them with other users' money. Under the simplest mixing method, an anonymity-craving user hands their bitcoins to a third-party address—a "tumbler" or "mixer"—which doles it back out to fresh, unsullied addresses belonging to the same owner. The mixer's address becomes a dead end in the trail, as the origins of any bitcoins emerging from it are indistinguishable from one another.

This method requires entrusting the potentially shady mixer with temporary ownership of the bitcoins. Less trust-dependent services, such as the JoinMarket mixer, act instead as matchmakers among many people looking to transfer bitcoins. By helping these parties merge their smaller transactions into one large transaction with many inputs and outputs, the mixer obscures who is paying whom.

Leaky Privacy Protection

The difficulty of anonymizing transactions got people thinking: Why not make anonymity a core cryptocurrency feature, rather than duct-taping it onto bitcoin? Monero, the digital currency the WannaCry culprits tried to convert their bitcoins into, is an alternative that effectively turns every transaction into a mix. Rather than recording a single sender, each blockchain entry records something akin to "one of the following six addresses sent a coin." Monero also offers "stealth addresses," which allow users to dissociate the addresses used in different transactions. After a few transactions have occurred, it becomes very difficult to track where the original money went.

Still, experts say the mouse has not yet escaped the cat. For one thing, ShapeShift, the service the WannaCry hackers used to exchange their bitcoins into monero, blacklisted the dirty bitcoin addresses from transacting on the service before most of the money could be traded. Additionally, ShapeShift publicly records which XMR (the unit of monero) were bought with which bitcoins, so investigators know where to start in the monero network.

Cybersecurity experts will likely discover more ways to de-anonymize downstream monero transactions. Andrew Miller, an assistant professor in computer science at the University of Illinois at Urbana–Champaign, points to a flaw in earlier versions of monero in which addresses with balances of zero would be included in mixes, effectively reducing the number of participants. Although that vulnerability has been fixed, he speculates there may be more like it. And because monero is not highly traded, there will be few legitimate users to give the thieves cover, Gronager adds.* Ultimately," says

Sarah Meiklejohn, an assistant professor of computer science at University College London, "however you move the money...it's going to be [in the blockchain] forever, so you're giving law enforcement a lot of time to figure it out."

Even if monero does sweep away the blockchain trail, the hackers will have countless opportunities to let their masks slip. Meiklejohn, who helped pioneer blockchain de-anonymization techniques, notes it is easy to spot when criminals reconsolidate money that has been split and handled by mixers. She has also managed to link thousands of unknown addresses with known dirty ones based on the fact that they regularly send money together.

In addition to the flow of money, Miller says, the crooks' network connections can give them away. If they are not exceptionally careful, law enforcement can see which computers are submitting the obfuscating transactions, which may be just the clue the FBI needs to launch a raid. Even the timing of transactions can be enough to reveal hidden connections between accounts. "If [the perpetrators] make even a single mistake, there may be enough information to track them," Miller says.

Ultimately, cryptocurrencies remain much like our familiar financial system. What really enable financial criminals, Gronager says, are jurisdictions willing to shelter them. But with many exchanges in such places facing either poor reputations or government takedowns, technological solutions will not save most swindlers from persistent investigators. Just as in the physical world, a perfect crime will be a rare beast—and WannaCry is likely no exception.

About the Author

Jesse Dunietz is a computer scientist and the Technology, Energy, and Society Fellow at Securing America's Future Energy (SAFE).

Women in Cybersecurity: Where We Are and Where We're Going

M eg Whitman, Ginni Rometty, Marissa Mayer and Safra Catz are among the few women who have broken the glass ceiling as CEOs of technology companies. However, while women make up half of the global population, we maintain significantly less representation at the C-Suite level in the technology field and particularly poor representation in cybersecurity. The cause of this may surprise you, but the solution doesn't require too much effort to implement.

In February 2018, Cybersecurity Ventures optimistically predicted that by the end of 2019, women will represent more than 20 percent of the global cybersecurity workforce. We're now only a few months away from that prediction either coming true or falling flat. Also noteworthy is the fact that the cybersecurity field still yearns for experts to join the workforce, whether they are male or female.

It's estimated that there will be a shortage of nearly two million cyber positions by the year 2022, and this shortage will increase over time unless radical and rapid change becomes a reality. Just take a look at the roster of any cybersecurity event anywhere in the world, and you will see the clear disparity in representation between males and females.

From Grade School Onward

Gender stereotyping from childhood plays a key role in the lack of women in cybersecurity. We must first overcome this challenge at home before overcoming male domination in the cybersecurity workforce.

- **Invest in STEM.** To encourage women to consider cybersecurity as a profession, our education system must offer opportunities for learning at least from middle school, if not through the entire K–12 journey. Federal governments can play a critical role in this journey by creating well-funded and tailored programs in science, technology, engineering and math (STEM) for our future young female population

Additionally, as a culture, we need to teach and practice that technology—inclusive of cybersecurity—is gender-neutral. Neither cybersecurity nor any line of code has any preference for gender. Participation in and contributions to STEM programs gives young girls a broad glimpse into the bright future, high potential and breadth of cybersecurity, and equally importantly, why this evolving field is so important in our increasingly interconnected lives.

- **Scholarships and role models.** In university, young female students can often be intimidated by the sheer number of male students in a technology-centric curriculum (or specific courses). Check out the statistics of the graduating class of any major university that offers engineering, science and/or technology degrees: the ratios are striking and significantly skewed. Many female students simply feel there is "no chance" for success in such male-dominated curricula and, as such, enroll with reservations because they have been compelled to do so. Consequently, they eventually never participate in the technology workforce or simply quit and enroll in disciplines that are not technology-related.

  We can overcome these fears by providing merit-based scholarships, co-op programs, academic incentives and workforce internships targeted to educate, excite and attract young females into technology-centric programs, and even more specifically for cybersecurity. This should become required coursework in the freshman year of any technology-centric university. By bringing women entrepreneurs in cybersecurity as guest speakers, lecturers and adjunct professors from the workforce in addition to recruiting more female professors, we can inspire young women to embark on technology-centric programs and degrees, which will help to prepare them better for the workforce and the lucrative field of cybersecurity.

- **Give them the experience: Hire a female intern!** Finally, as proposed above, we need to hire more female interns starting with high school students and especially into the university years to give them an opportunity in cybersecurity, no matter how simple or advanced the internship or co-op.

   Of course, hiring must be based not only on merit but also on the curiosity, drive and passion of the individual. During the internship, mentorship by female executives who have "been there, done that" can play a significant role in inspiration, talent recognition and eventual workforce retention. The network externality effect of female teenagers should never be underestimated!

- **Continuous fostering is needed.** Inspiring more women to enter cybersecurity is the first challenge. Next, the ability to excel and break through the glass ceiling, which is real and undeniable in the male-dominated cybersecurity workforce. Here are my thoughts on climbing the corporate ladder no matter how small or large the organization.

Let's Smash the Glass Ceiling Together

Women have to work twice as hard because of our role and responsibility in life outside of the workforce. I speak from experience as I am the mother of two children who not only look up to me but also depend on me. So how can you or your organization help?

- **Acknowledge the gap.** We have a problem with gender equality in this country. Recognize this gap, and set monthly, quarterly and annual goals to close this gap in whichever manner makes sense to your organization.
- **Conduct positive discrimination through recruiting.** Simply put, we need to recruit more women. Call it what it is, positive discrimination, to balance out our industry. Look, this is the

natural course of correction if you want to get to equality. Yes, I know it is challenging especially since the pipeline is sparse; however, we need to start and keep at it. Engage support organizations that are focused on women in cybersecurity. They exist and are already making headway; for example, see Alta Associates and the EWF, and talk to any of the women who are involved in any capacity with these organizations to better understand what support groups such as these can do for you.

- **Mentorship matters.** Leverage women leaders and those upcoming in cybersecurity today as role models. Make a concerted effort to promote the trailblazers who are already in your workforce, but don't forget to train, coach and mentor new entrants who can also eventually reach the pinnacle of leadership and technical prowess.

- **Make equality a responsibility.** Equality is a moral responsibility and has to be a genuine effort by the leaders in your organization. Equality cannot just be an HR or CEO agenda line item. Nor can it be just a numbers game. It has to become a pervasive cultural responsibility that is sourced from our mind and heart. If you are a man or woman, it is your moral responsibility to speak up if you see inequality and to help those just starting out in their career by making a concerted effort to grow your female peers into positions of technical and business leadership that will eventually bring balance and sustainability to your organization. Remember what I said: positive discrimination.

Where Do We Go from Here?

It continues to be a slow process, but our society must change its perception of women at the outset. STEM is gender-neutral and must be made available for everyone. Cybersecurity is also gender-neutral and can be taught from an early age. Leadership in technology and business is equally gender-neutral as well. Let's nurture opportunities for women early and equally as we do for men today.

At the end of the day, diversity drives creativity. Men and women each bring their own unique skill sets to the workforce and today's cybersecurity workforce requires a holistic, analytical and diverse skill set. This makes women a key asset to the organization and EQUAL to men.

Yes, as women, we like to say that we are more supportive, analytical, persuasive, have better intuition and are more detailed oriented than men. But for now, let's start with nurturing the opportunities available and create equality instead of tagging who is better at what because goodness is not gender, race, religion or country of origin. Goodness is goodness and works best when we are whole and working together as one team.

We have made some progress towards gender parity over the last 100 years but are still struggling in economics, education, technology and political systems. We have a long journey ahead of us, perhaps another 100 years! I want to augment my role model, the Notorious RBG. Women will have achieved true equality when men share with them the responsibility of bringing up the next generation and in a 40-year span we have four to five female presidents.

I was fortunate that I was given a chance to work in cybersecurity. We all need to continue to promote females in cybersecurity, and I am 100 percent confident that more women will scale to greater heights if we are simply given the opportunity early on in our lives.

About the Author

Nahal Shahidzadeh is co-founder and COO at Acceptto. She is also an entrepreneur with broad experience covering financial services and managing private funds. Previously, she worked on microprocessor design and development of the Pentium 4 microprocessor at Intel Corp. with eight issued and pending patents.

Section 6: Protecting Your Privacy

6.1 Congressional Ignorance Leaves the U.S. Vulnerable
     to Cyberthreats
     By Jackson Barnett

6.2 Misdiagnosing Our Cyberhealth
     By Emily Balcetis

6.3 Passwords Are on the Way Out, and It's about Time
     By David Pogue

6.4 Social Security Numbers Aren't Secure: What Should We
     Use Instead?
     By Sophie Bushwick

6.5 The Mathematics of (Hacking) Passwords
     By Jean-Paul Delahaye

6.6 How Cryptojacking Can Corrupt the Internet of Things
     By Larry Greenemeier

Congressional Ignorance Leaves the U.S. Vulnerable to Cyberthreats

By Jackson Barnett

In the 2016 U.S. presidential election, Russian hackers penetrated Illinois's voter-registration database, viewing voters' addresses and parts of their social security numbers. Election results were not affected, but the attack put intruders in the position to alter voter data, according to a report from the Senate Select Committee on Intelligence. The incursion was part of hacking attempts against all 50 states, and intruders will try even more vigorously in 2020, yet experts say Congress is doing little to improve defenses. The Brennan Center for Justice at New York University says states will need just more than $2.1 billion to upgrade election computer systems, yet last month the Senate approved only a fraction of that amount: $250 million.

One reason for the inadequate response is that elected representatives and their staffs are not tech savvy enough to understand the scope of the problems, says Lawrence Norden, director of the Election Reform Program at the Brennan Center and co-author of the cost analysis. His sentiments are echoed by other cybersecurity specialists. "I just didn't have the tools," recalls Meg King, director of the Digital Futures Project at the Woodrow Wilson International Center for Scholars, who worked on a cyberdefense bill a decade ago as a senior staff member on a House homeland security subcommittee. She now describes that bill as "too little, too late." Today her think tank has begun to offer staffers short courses in cybersecurity issues, but security researchers worry that step will not be enough.

While substantially changing the outcome of an election by hacking into voting machines is extremely unlikely because those machines and the ballot counting process are very decentralized, altering voter rolls could block people from voting. If the system is

123

even slightly exploited, says David Becker, executive director of the Center for Election Innovation & Research, it could trigger public distrust in elections. "I think the greatest challenge that we do have is to make sure that we maintain the integrity of our election system," said Joseph Maguire, the U.S. acting director of national intelligence, during recent congressional testimony.

Because election security is so important to democracy, Norden wants Congress to fund new state offices that can act as cyber-response teams when attackers try to breach or even alter voter roll information. Yet this project is one that Republican Senate Majority Leader Mitch McConnell of Kentucky has been uninterested in pursuing, arguing that such responsibility rests with the states themselves. But the funding that state governments have allocated, along with federal assistance, to date "only scratches the surface," Becker says. Continuous election security for the future means supporting states with money to update systems that store voter information and to improve cybersecurity training, he adds. "We need to address this as an ongoing expense," Becker says.

King says one reason Capitol Hill keeps proposing solutions that fall short of the problem is high staff turnover, which means knowledge evaporates when people leave. Further, institutions that provide nonpartisan information to Congress, such as the Congressional Research Service, are stretched thin. The Office of Technology Assessment, a Congressional service that was intended to advise lawmakers on science and technology issues, was shut down in 1995. Recently representatives from both parties have begun efforts to resurrect it, but support has yet to materialize into real funding.

To get staffers to better understand the threats and how to find the right solutions to technical problems such as election security, the Wilson Center established the Congressional Cybersecurity Lab under the umbrella of King's Digital Futures Project. The lab offers weekly seminars led by technologists and runs hands-on exercises over a six-week period. After staffers complete the program, they have access to a pool of experts to advise them "without a lobbyist's perspective," King says, as well as a network of lab alumni. Knowledge gained by staffers, she adds, should let them craft more effective legislation and communicate more easily with independent cybersecurity researchers at universities and corporations.

Legislators have a vested interest in supporting more secure elections and more cybersecurity expertise on Capitol Hill, points out Kathryn Waldron, a cybersecurity researcher at the R Street Institute. As 2020 campaigns gear up, hacking attempts against politicians and their offices will likely increase, she says. "It is not just a threat to national security; it is threat to American democracy at large," Waldron says.

About the Author

Jackson Barnett is a Colorado-based journalist who has written for Scientific American, FedScoop, *The Boston Herald,* The Denver Post, *and numerous other outlets..*

Misdiagnosing Our Cyberhealth

By Emily Balcetis

As schools and universities closed across the country, the #ClassOf2020 challenge went viral, with graduates taking to social media platforms such as Facebook, Instagram and Twitter to mark the rite of passage online. Using the hashtag, they posted photographs of themselves in cap and gown, holding their diploma and surrounded by loved ones. Millions of people shared #ClassOf2020 images, which included smiling selfies taken in graduation regalia, proud parents hugging their children, fizzing bottles of champagne and tassels flying high above caps tossed in the air. It was a moment of joy captured amid global crisis.

But these snapshots may have also given cybercriminals valuable information and insight into the private lives of these recent graduates. Using the hashtag, hackers could have mined the posts for information on the students, from the diploma in their hand to the university painted on their cap and the pets and family members tagged in the background. What few of them realized was that the content of these photographs and captions also held the answers to the security questions designed to protect their accounts. A quick scroll through Instagram, and the answer to "What's your pet's name?" or "What high school did you attend?" can go from a shot in the dark to an educated guess. As the Better Business Bureau has warned, posters may not realize that the content of these photographs and captions also held the answers to the security questions designed to protect their accounts. Hackers can cross-reference information posted to these social media campaigns against other publicly available personal data to glean our birth date, hometown, and other key facts that can be used to change our passwords and take over our accounts.

We hear a lot about what we can do to be cybersafe. We know to be wary about what we download. We know passwords should include random strings of letters, numbers and symbols. But what we don't realize is that our human psychology is working against us, lulling us into a false sense of security. We think of ourselves as less vulnerable than others. We disregard people's experiences and testimonies when considering our own risk.

In three pilot experiments, I and my colleagues investigated how individuals determine their risk of succumbing to cyberattack. Before reporting their own or others' likelihood of falling victim to an attempted scam, all subjects received base rates—the percentage of people who clicked on an e-mail link or downloaded an attachment sent by an unknown or suspicious source. Our research found that while participants used these percentages when assessing others' risk, they largely ignored them when considering their own, suggesting a startling cognitive bias. We misjudge our own vulnerability, because we believe that, whatever the rule, we are somehow the exception.

Hackers take advantage of our complacency. In 2017 the Poneman Institute reported on the cost of data breaches in 13 countries and regions. According to its analysis, U.S. organizations pay the highest price for data breaches, with average annual losses of $4.13 million because of customer turnovers, reputation losses and diminished goodwill. When probing why, the researchers estimated that about half of the cost of U.S. breaches was the result of human error or negligence.

How do we prevent this problem? One approach is to motivate people through fear. Yan Chen of Auburn University at Montgomery and Fatemeh Zahedi of the University of Wisconsin–Milwaukee conducted a survey and found that when people in China and the U.S. had greater fear that they might be susceptible to a serious cyberattack, they more frequently asked for professional help and took precautions to protect against security breaches. Aligning with this evidence, experts believe that to increase the fear and awareness of the dangers of cyberattacks, they should report shocking statistics about them and the stories of victims' experiences.

There's reason to believe this strategy might work. Supposedly, social learning—where we view the good and bad outcomes others' experience—is one of the most effective forms of education and prevention. We can learn more, and do so faster, by observing others, using their experience to inform our own decisions. If we want to know the likelihood that we could be targeted, we should draw from what other people did and the consequences they faced. But what my team's research suggests is that when it comes to cyberthreat, we don't learn from others.

This "scared straight" approach often falls short, because, quite often, we simply ignore the message. Seeing the base rates does little to change people's beliefs about their own vulnerability to an attack. In one of our studies, we recruited 432 adults across the country and had them report the probability that they would respond to different illegitimate phishing scams that asked them to disclose personal information in exchange for something they wanted. For example, respondents considered how likely they were to click on a link to complete a survey in exchange for a chance to win a new Apple Watch. On average, participants estimated there was a 13 percent chance they would respond as requested. When asked to predict the likelihood of someone else doing so, however, their estimates were 46 percent higher, rising to about 19 percent. The subjects expected other people to be more likely to respond to the request, and as a result, they underestimated their own risk.

In assessing their own vulnerability, individuals did not consult the group averages. The participants received true base rates about the percent of people who clicked a suspicious link, downloaded an attachment from an unknown sender or completed one of the other tasks listed in the e-mail. For every 10 percent increase in the actual likelihood reported in the base rates, self-predictions rose by only 3.5 percent, whereas predictions made about others did so by 8 percent.

Despite the increase in group averages, the self-assessments stayed the same, largely because people didn't even look at the base rates. Embedded in the frame of the computer monitor were four infrared sensors tracking each participant's gaze. Using this technology, we measured how often people looked at the base rates and found that they glanced at the group averages 12 percent less frequently when predicting their own reactions than when predicting other peoples'. They considered the general averages useful when thinking about someone else but less important when thinking about themselves.

People often have access to base rates but disregard them. This pattern has led prominent theorists to propose that our disinterest in other people's experiences reflects a more general cognitive bias. Psychologists Nicholas Epley and David Dunning, for instance, found that when individuals considered whether they were likely to donate to a charity, their predictions did not track population base rates of such donations.

Our belief in our own exceptionalism makes us less informed about our own vulnerabilities online. So how can we override our tendency to disregard others' experiences? First, we can assess our risk with an impartial eye, weighing the statistics over our personal beliefs. We can review security settings on social media and limit access to our posts. We can change our security questions and pick answers that can't be found on the Internet. And, most importantly, we can learn from our mistakes. Because once we've become one of the statistics, we aren't likely to overlook them again.

About the Author

Emily Balcetis is an associate professor of psychology at New York University and author of Clearer, Closer, Better: How Successful People See the World.

Passwords Are on the Way Out, and It's about Time

O ur tech lives are full of pain points, but at least the world's tech geniuses seem committed to solving them. Today who complains about the things that bugged us a decade ago, such as heavy laptops, slow cellular Internet, the inability to do e-mail in planes?

It was only a matter of time before those geniuses started tackling one of the longest-running pain points in history: passwords. We're supposed to create a long, complex, unguessable password—capital and lowercase letters, numbers and symbols, with a few Arabic letters thrown in if possible. *For each site*. Don't reuse a password. Oh, and change them all every month.

Sorry, security experts. Not possible. Not for an average person, not even for you. Nobody has that kind of memory.

To make matters worse, passwords aren't even especially secure. See any recent headline about stolen passwords or about some company's servers being hacked.

It's time to kill the password.

Surely, in the 50 years since we started typing passwords, somebody must have invented a better security system. The answer: yes and no. Apps such as 1Password and Dashlane memorize and enter long, complicated passwords *for* you. But most of them cost money, they don't work on every Web account and the nontechie public doesn't know they exist.

There's also two-factor authentication, which makes you type a password *and* a code texted to your phone to log in. It's an unbelievable hassle. The masses will never go for it.

Finally, biometric approaches can be both secure and easy because they recognize us, not memorized strings of text. Here there's hope. Fingerprint readers on smartphones, tablets and laptops are becoming common, cheap, convenient and essentially impossible to hack on a large scale. So far they're primarily useful for logging us into our *machines*. Shouldn't the next step be letting us log into our Web accounts? Iris scanning is another biometric technology, fast enough to work well at automated border-crossing systems and secure enough for national ID programs such as India's (it's enrolling 1.2 billion people).

At the moment, iris scanners are far too new and expensive to build into every phone and laptop—but almost every technology gets cheaper over time. Some scanners can be fooled by a photograph of your eye, but this problem, too, can be overcome (by tracking your pupil as you read something, for example). Bottom line: there's no insurmountable problem in iris reading's future.

Same with voice authentication, using the unique pitch, accent and frequencies of your speaking voice as your key. It's cheap enough for wide adoption—our phones and gadgets already have microphones. Worried about bad guys faking out the system with a recording of your voice? That can't happen if the phrase you're asked to speak changes every time you log in.

The only roadblocks here are background noise and laryngitis. And as with any biometric security solution, this approach really requires a backup system—like a password—just in case.

Then there's Windows Hello, a new feature of Windows 10 that lets you log in with fingerprint, iris or facial recognition—whatever your laptop is equipped to handle. The face option is especially exciting. You just sit down at the computer, and it unlocks instantly. You can't fool it with a photograph or even a 3-D model of your head, because the Intel RealSense camera it requires includes infrared and 3-D sensors.

Of course, very few gadgets come with that camera preinstalled. But the RealSense concept is truly the Holy Grail: secure and convenient. If the hardware ever became as ubiquitous and cheap as, say, our phones' fingerprint readers, we could have a winner.

Clearly, the password concept is broken. Equally clearly, these new technologies can provide both the security and the convenience the world demands. Nothing's quite there yet, and we need to keep our eye on privacy concerns (who owns the databases of biometric scans, for example?).

But one thing is for sure: this is one pain point that's got everyone's attention.

About the Author

David Pogue is the anchor columnist for Yahoo Tech and host of several NOVA miniseries on PBS.

Social Security Numbers Aren't Secure: What Should We Use Instead?

By Sophie Bushwick

Telecommunications company T-Mobile confirmed last month that hackers gained access to 54 million users' personal data, including names, addresses, dates of birth and—perhaps worst of all—social security numbers. The latter are a big score for identity thieves because they can be used to unlock financial services, government benefits and private medical information.

This is only the latest major data breach to expose such identifying information on a massive scale, rendering hundreds of millions of Americans more vulnerable to identity theft. To stem the problem, some experts are calling for an end to social security numbers, suggesting we should replace them with some other—and less inherently vulnerable—way of proving one's identity. But security experts think the government does not need to entirely do away with them. Instead the organizations that use social security numbers as proof of identity must start requiring more than a single form of ID.

The Federal Trade Commission recorded 1.4 million reports of identity theft in 2020, and that year such fraud cost victims an estimated $56 billion, according to financial consulting firm Javelin Strategy & Research. Identity thieves might use a variety of information to impersonate individuals, but one of the best keys for accessing money is the social security number, or SSN. This string of nine digits, which the federal government started issuing in 1936, was originally assigned to people simply to determine their social security benefits.

"It was not set up to be this universal, unique identifier," explains Eva Velasquez, president and CEO of the Identity Theft Resource Center, a nonprofit organization that supports victims of such crimes. But eventually, the lifetime number became a convenient way for people to apply for credit cards, student loans, mortgages and other lines of credit—among other services. "Often [SSNs can be used to] get medical goods or services, and that includes prescriptions, durable medical equipment and things of that nature," Velasquez says. "And then, of course, [they are used to apply for] government benefits: things like unemployment, SNAP [Supplemental Nutrition Assistance Program] benefits, aid to families with dependent children." Access to such a wide range of assets makes the numbers a prime target for hackers.

With tens of millions of SSNs now exposed by data breaches, a number of politicians and security experts have called for companies to phase out the use of these identifiers. In 2017 Rob Joyce, then cybersecurity coordinator at the White House and now director of cybersecurity at the National Security Agency, suggested replacing the social security number with a harder-to-crack option: a much longer string of characters known as a cryptographic key. But any lone number, whether it has nine digits or 100, could still be stolen from a repository and shared online. "As soon as you develop or create another static, unique identifier, it's just going to be another number that you issue to everyone," Velasquez says. "Then that becomes valuable to the thief, so they will target the systems that have that data."

Modern technology has enabled other ways to verify identity: A password manager can generate a long, hard-to-guess password for each account, and this type of program often makes it easy to change those passwords in the event of a data breach. A USB key can be plugged into a computer to authenticate its owner. Biometric information, such as a fingerprint or face, can be scanned by a smartphone. But experts do not recommend replacing the social security number with any one of these methods alone; the most secure option is to protect identity with multiple factors. "Instead of focusing our security risks on this single data point, we need to develop these more holistic and multilayered approaches to identity management," Velasquez says. "So if any one or two elements of that identity are compromised, it doesn't compromise the entire identity."

The practice of proving one's identity by providing a fact one knows, such as a social security number, is called knowledge-based authentication, or KBA. And it is extremely vulnerable to hackers because all they need to impersonate someone is to steal that particular tidbit of knowledge, explains Rachel Tobac, an ethical hacker and CEO of SocialProof Security, an organization that helps companies spot potential vulnerabilities to cyberattacks. "For instance, it can be solicited out of you and stolen by a social engineer. It can be involved in a breach and dumped publicly online when a company that you trust with your KBA ... [is] hit with a cyberattack," she says. Some types of KBA, such as birthdays or mothers' maiden names, may even appear on social media for anyone to find. Technically, a password is another form of KBA, Tobac adds—but if a password is stolen, it can be reset. "I can't just go ahead and change my birthday, my social security number, my address every time a Web site or an institution that I trust with that information has a cybersecurity incident," she points out.

For effective multifactor authentication, or MFA, it is not enough to simply require two or more pieces of knowledge. After all, breaches like the recent one at T-Mobile release a variety of data about each victim. Instead, Tobac says, the other factors should come from a different source: something you *have* or something you *are*. The former category might include a physical USB key or a even a phone, which can receive a text message with a unique one-time code. The latter category encompasses physical traits, which can be measured by biometric scans. For instance, a multifactor authentication process might require a person to enter their social security number and follow up with a code word texted to their phone. Another version might involve them entering a password and then scanning their fingerprint.

Not even multifactor authentication provides perfect security, though. A determined hacker might use a SIM-swapping technique to transfer your phone number to another device, allowing them to intercept the text message that was supposed to provide a second layer of security. A biometric scan can be fooled. But by requiring multiple forms of authentication, a system creates a lot more friction for malicious actors. "I can't sit here and tell you that this method is going to be 100 percent fail-safe," Tobac says. "But for most people, with most threat models, it's going to stop the attackers."

Despite its strength, multifactor authentication is far from being universally required. Some credit bureaus, customer support hotlines, government accounts and other services continue to rely on simple knowledge-based authentication such as a social security number. But the more secure approach is gradually becoming more popular. "We're already on that track. We're seeing movement in that direction," Velasquez says, pointing out that the U.S. federal government, financial industry and tech companies are beginning to require multiple layers of authentication. Tobac agrees. "I can see that the wheels are turning. They're not turning fast enough, but they are turning," she says. "And I think we have to continue to put pressure on the companies that we all rely on to protect our data, our security, our privacy, to move from KBA to MFA flow."

About the Author

Sophie Bushwick is an associate editor covering technology at Scientific American.

The Mathematics of (Hacking) Passwords

By Jean-Paul Delahaye

At one time or another, we have all been frustrated by trying to set a password, only to have it rejected as too weak. We are also told to change our choices regularly. Obviously such measures add safety, but how exactly?

I will explain the mathematical rationale for some standard advice, including clarifying why six characters are not enough for a good password and why you should never use only lowercase letters. I will also explain how hackers can uncover passwords even when stolen data sets lack them.

ChOose#W!sely@*

Here is the logic behind setting hack-resistant passwords. When you are asked to create a password of a certain length and combination of elements, your choice will fit into the realm of all unique options that conform to that rule—into the "space" of possibilities. For example, if you were told to use six lowercase letters—such as, afzjxd, auntie, secret, wwwwww—the space would contain 26^6, or 308,915,776, possibilities. In other words, there are 26 possible choices for the first letter, 26 possible choices for the second, and so forth. These choices are independent: you do not have to use different letters, so the size of the password space is the product of the possibilities, or $26 \times 26 \times 26 \times 26 \times 26 \times 26 = 26^6$.

If you are told to select a 12-character password that can include uppercase and lowercase letters, the 10 digits and 10 symbols (say, !, @, #, $, %, ^, &, ?, / and +), you would have 72 possibilities for each of the 12 characters of the password. The size of the possibility space would then be 72^{12} (19,408,409,961,765,342,806,016, or close to 19×10^{21}).

That is more than 62 trillion times the size of the first space. A computer running through all the possibilities for your 12-character password one by one would take 62 trillion times longer. If your computer spent a second visiting the six-character space, it would have to devote two million years to examining each of the passwords in the 12-character space. The multitude of possibilities makes it impractical for a hacker to carry out a plan of attack that might have been feasible for the six-character space.

Calculating the size of these spaces by computer usually involves counting the number of binary digits in the number of possibilities. That number, N, is derived from this formula: $1 + \text{integer}(\log_2(N))$. In the formula, the value of $\log_2(N)$ is a real number with many decimal places, such as $\log_2(26^6) = 28.202638....$ The "integer" in the formula indicates that the decimal portion of that log value is omitted, rounding down to a whole number—as in integer(28.202638... 28). For the example of six lowercase letters above, the computation results in 29 bits; for the more complex, 12-character example, it is 75 bits. (Mathematicians refer to the possibility spaces as having entropy of 29 and 75 bits, respectively.) The French National Cybersecurity Agency (ANSSI) recommends spaces having a minimum of 100 bits when it comes to passwords or secret keys for encryption systems that absolutely must be secure. Encryption involves representing data in a way that ensures it cannot be retrieved unless a recipient has a secret code-breaking key. In fact, the agency recommends a possibility space of 128 bits to guarantee security for several years. It considers 64 bits to be very small (very weak); 64 to 80 bits to be small; and 80 to 100 bits to be medium (moderately strong).

Moore's law (which says that the computer-processing power available at a certain price doubles roughly every two years) explains why a relatively weak password will not suffice for long-term use: over time computers using brute force can find passwords faster. Although the pace of Moore's law appears to be decreasing, it is wise to take it into account for passwords that you hope will remain secure for a long time.

For a truly strong password as defined by ANSSI, you would need, say, a sequence of 16 characters, each taken from a set of 200 characters. This would make a 123-bit space, which would render the password close to impossible to memorize. Therefore, system designers are generally less demanding and accept low- or medium-strength passwords. They insist on long ones only when the passwords are automatically generated by the system, and users do not have to remember them.

There are other ways to guard against password cracking. The simplest is well known and used by credit cards: after three unsuccessful attempts, access is blocked. Alternative ideas have also been suggested, such as doubling the waiting time after each successive failed attempt but allowing the system to reset after a long period, such as 24 hours. These methods, however, are ineffective when an attacker is able to access the system without being detected or if the system cannot be configured to interrupt and disable failed attempts.

How Long Does It Take to Search All Possible Passwords?

For a password to be difficult to crack, it should be chosen randomly from a large set, or "space," of possibilities. The size, T, of the possibility space is based on the length, A, of the list of valid characters in the password and the number of characters, N, in the password. The size of this space ($T = A^N$) may vary considerably. Each of the following examples specifies values of A, N, T and the number of hours, D, that hackers would have to spend to try every permutation of characters one by one. X is the number of years that will have to pass before the space can be checked in less than one hour, assuming that Moore's law (the doubling of computing capacity every two years) remains valid. I also assume that in 2019, a computer can explore a billion possibilities per second. I represent this set of assumptions with the following three relationships and consider five possibilities based on values of A and N:

RELATIONSHIPS

$T = A^N$

$D = T/(109 \times 3{,}600)$

$X = 2 \log_2[T/(109 \times 3{,}600)]$

RESULTS

If $A = 26$ and $N = 6$, then $T = 308{,}915{,}776$

$D = 0.0000858$ computing hour

$X = 0$; it is already possible to crack all passwords in the space in under an hour

---

If $A = 26$ and $N = 12$, then $T = 9.5 \times 10^{16}$

$D = 26{,}508$ computing hours

$X = 29$ years before passwords can be cracked in under an hour

---

If $A = 100$ and $N = 10$, then $T = 10^{20}$

$D = 27{,}777{,}777$ computing hours

$X = 49$ years before passwords can be cracked in under an hour

---

If $A = 100$ and $N = 15$, then $T = 10^{30}$

$D = 2.7 \times 10^{17}$ computing hours

$X = 115$ years before passwords can be cracked in under an hour

---

If $A = 200$ and $N = 20$, then $T = 1.05 \times 10^{46}$

$D = 2.7 \times 10^{33}$ computing hours

$X = 222$ years before passwords can be cracked in under an hour

---

Weaponizing Dictionaries and Other Hacker Tricks

Quite often an attacker succeeds in obtaining encrypted passwords or password "fingerprints" (which I will discuss more fully later)

from a system. If the hack has not been detected, the interloper may have days or even weeks to attempt to derive the actual passwords.

To understand the subtle processes exploited in such cases, take another look at the possibility space. When I spoke earlier of bit size and password space (or entropy), I implicitly assumed that the user consistently chooses passwords at random. But typically the choice is not random: people tend to select a password they can remember (locomotive) rather than an arbitrary string of characters (xdichqewax).

This practice poses a serious problem for security because it makes passwords vulnerable to so-called dictionary attacks. Lists of commonly used passwords have been collected and classified according to how frequently they are used. Attackers attempt to crack passwords by going through these lists systematically. This method works remarkably well because, in the absence of specific constraints, people naturally choose simple words, surnames, first names and short sentences, which considerably limits the possibilities. In other words, the nonrandom selection of passwords essentially reduces possibility space, which decreases the average number of attempts needed to uncover a password.

Below are the first 25 entries in one of these password dictionaries, listed in order, starting with the most common one. (I took the examples from a database of five million passwords that was leaked in 2017 and analyzed by SplashData.)

1. 123456
2. password
3. 12345678
4. qwerty
5. 12345
6. 123456789
7. letmein
8. 1234567
9. football

10. iloveyou

11. admin

12. welcome

13. monkey

14. login

15. abc123

16. starwars

17. 123123

18. dragon

19. passw0rd

20. master

21. hello

22. freedom

23. whatever

24. qazwsx

25. trustno1

If you use password or iloveyou, you are not as clever as you thought! Of course, lists differ according to the country where they are collected and the Web sites involved; they also vary over time.

For four-digit passwords (for example, the PIN code of SIM cards on smartphones), the results are even less imaginative. In 2013, based on a collection of 3.4 million passwords each containing four digits, the DataGenetics Web site reported that the most commonly used four-digit sequence (representing 11 percent of choices) was 1234, followed by 1111 (6 percent) and 0000 (2 percent). The least-used four-digit password was 8068. Careful, though, this ranking may no longer be true now that the result has been published. The 8068 choice appeared only 25 times among the 3.4-million four-digit sequences in the database, which is much less than the 340 uses that would have occurred if each four-digit combination had been used with the same frequency. The first 20 series of four digits are: 1234; 1111; 0000; 1212; 7777; 1004; 2000; 4444; 2222; 6969; 9999; 3333; 5555; 6666; 1122; 1313; 8888; 4321; 2001; 1010.

Even without a password dictionary, using differences in frequency of letter use (or double letters) in a language makes it possible to plan an effective attack. Some attack methods also take into account that, to facilitate memorization, people may choose passwords that have a certain structure—such as A1=B2=C3, AwX2AwX2 or O0o.lli. (which I used for a long time)—or that are derived by combining several simple strings, such as password123 or johnABC0000. Exploiting such regularities makes it possible to for hackers to speed up detection.

Making Hash of Hackers

As the main text explains, instead of storing clients' passwords, Internet servers store the "fingerprints" of these passwords: sequences of characters that are derived from the passwords. In the event of an attack, the use of fingerprints can make it is very difficult, if not impossible, for hackers to use what they find.

The transformation is achieved by using algorithms known as cryptographic hash functions. These are meticulously developed processes that transform a data file, F, however long it may be, into a sequence, $h(F)$, called a fingerprint of F. For example, the hash function SHA256 transforms the phrase "Nice weather" into:
DB0436DB78280F3B45C2E09654522197D59EC98E7E64AEB967A2A19EF7C394A3

(64 hexadecimal, or base 16, characters, which is equivalent to 256 bits)

Changing a single character in the file completely alters its fingerprint. For example, if the first character of Nice weather is changed to lowercase (nice weather), the hash SHA256 will generate another fingerprint:
02C532E7418CD1B57961A1B090DB6EC37B3C58380AC0E6877F3B6155C974647E

You can do these calculations yourself and check them at https://passwordsgenerator.net/sha256-hash-generator or www.xorbin.com/tools/sha256-hash-calculator

Good hash functions produce fingerprints that are similar to those that would be obtained if the fingerprint sequence was uniformly chosen at random. In particular, for any possible random result (a sequence of 64 hexadecimal characters), it is impossible to find a data file F with this fingerprint in a reasonable amount of time.

There have been several generations of hash functions. The SHA0 and SHA1 generations are obsolete and are not recommended. The SHA2 generation, including SHA256, is considered secure.

The Take-Home for Consumers

Taking all this into account, properly designed Web sites analyze the passwords proposed at the time of their creation and reject those that would be too easy to recover. It is irritating, but it's for your own good.

The obvious conclusion for users is that they must choose their passwords randomly. Some software does provide a random password. Be aware, however, that such password-generating software may, deliberately or not, use a poor pseudo-random generator, in which case what it provides may be imperfect.

You can check whether any of your passwords has already been hacked by using a Web tool called Pwned Passwords (https://haveibeenpwned.com/Passwords). Its database includes more than 500 million passwords obtained after various attacks.

I tried e=mc2e=mc2, which I liked and believed to be secure, and received an unsettling response: "This password has been seen 114 times before." Additional attempts show that it is difficult to come up with easy-to-memorize passwords that the database does not know. For example, aaaaaa appeared 395,299 times; a1b2c3d4, 113,550 times; abcdcba, 378 times; abczyx, 186 times; acegi, 117 times; clinton, 18,869 times; bush, 3,291 times; obama, 2,391 times; trump, 859 times.

It is still possible to be original. The Web site did not recognize the following six passwords, for example: eyahaled (my name spelled backward); bizzzzard; meaudepace and modeuxpass (two puns on the French for "password"); abcdef2019; passwaurde. Now that I've tried them, I wonder if the database will add them when it next updates. In that case, I won't use them.

Advice for Web Sites

Web sites, too, follow various rules of thumb. The National Institute of Standards and Technology recently published a notice recommending the use of dictionaries to filter users' password choices.

Among the rules that a good Web server designer absolutely must adhere to is, do not store plaintext lists of usernames and passwords on the computer used to operate the Web site.

The reason is obvious: hackers could access the computer containing this list, either because the site is poorly protected or because the system or processor contains a serious flaw unknown to anyone except the attackers (a so-called zero-day flaw), who can exploit it.

One alternative is to encrypt the passwords on the server: use a secret code that transforms them via an encryption key into what will appear to be random character sequences to anyone who does not possess the decryption key. This method works, but it has two disadvantages. First, it requires decrypting the stored password every time to compare it with the user's entry, which is inconvenient. Second, and more seriously, the decryption necessary for this comparison requires storing the decryption key in the Web site computer's memory. This key may therefore be detected by an attacker, which brings us back to the original problem.

A better way to store passwords is through what are called hash functions that produce "fingerprints." For any data in a file—symbolized as F—a hash function generates a fingerprint. (The process is also called condensing or hashing.) The fingerprint—$h(F)$—is a fairly short word associated with F but produced in such a way that, in practice, it is impossible to deduce F from $h(F)$. Hash functions are said to be one-way: getting from F to $h(F)$ is easy;

getting from h(F) to F is practically impossible. In addition, the hash functions used have the characteristic that even if it is possible for two data inputs, F and F', to have the same fingerprint (known as a collision), in practice for a given F, it is almost impossible to find an F' with a fingerprint identical to F.

Using such hash functions allows passwords to be securely stored on a computer. Instead of storing the list of paired usernames and passwords, the server stores only the list of username/fingerprint pairs.

When a user wishes to connect, the server will read the individual's password, compute the fingerprint and determine whether it corresponds to the list of stored username/fingerprint pairs associated with that username. That maneuver frustrates hackers because even if they have managed to access the list, they will be unable to derive the users' passwords, inasmuch as it is practically impossible to go from fingerprint to password. Nor can they generate another password with an identical fingerprint to fool the server because it is practically impossible to create collisions.

Still, no approach is foolproof, as is highlighted by frequent reports of the hacking of major sites. In 2016, for example, data from a billion accounts were stolen from Yahoo!

For added safety, a method known as salting is sometimes used to further impede hackers from exploiting stolen lists of username/fingerprint pairs. Salting is the addition of a unique random string of characters to each password. It ensures that even if two users employ the same password, the stored fingerprints will differ. The list on the server will contain three components for each user: username, fingerprint derived after salt was added to the password, and the salt itself. When the server checks the password entered by a user, it adds the salt, computes the fingerprint and compares the result with its database.

Even when user passwords are weak, this method considerably complicates the hacker's work. Without salting, a hacker can compute all the fingerprints in a dictionary and see those in the stolen data;

all the passwords in the hacker's dictionary can be identified. With salting, for every salt used, the hacker must compute the salted fingerprints of all the passwords in the hacker's dictionary. For a set of 1,000 users, this multiplies by 1,000 the computations required to use the hacker's dictionary.

Survival of the Fittest

It goes without saying that hackers have their own ways of fighting back. They face a dilemma, though: their simplest options either take a lot of computing power or a lot of memory. Often neither option is viable. There is, however, a compromise approach known as the rainbow table method (see "Rainbow Tables Help Hackers").

In the age of the Internet, supercomputers and computer networks, the science of password setting and cracking continues to evolve—as does the relentless struggle between those who strive to protect passwords and those who are determined to steal, and potentially abuse, them.

Rainbow Tables Help Hackers

Say you are a hacker looking to exploit data that you have acquired. These data consist of username/fingerprint pairs, and you know the hash function (see "Making Hash of Hackers"). The password is contained in the possibility space of strings of 12 lowercase letters, which corresponds to 56 bits of information and 26^{12} (9.54×10^{16}) possible passwords.

At least two strong approaches are open to you:

Method 1. You scroll through the entire space of passwords. You calculate the fingerprint, $h(P)$, for each password, checking to see whether it appears in the stolen data. You do not need a lot of memory, because prior results are deleted with each new attempt, although you do, of course, have to keep track of the possibilities that have been tested.

Scrolling through all the possible passwords in this way takes a long time. If your computer runs a billion tests per second, you will need $26^{12}/(10^9 \times 3{,}600 \times 24)$ days (1,104 days), or about three years to complete the task. The feat is not impossible; if you happen to have a computer network of 1,000 machines, one day will suffice. It is not feasible, however, to repeat such a calculation every time you wish to test additional data, such as if you obtain a new set of username/fingerprint pairs. (Because you have not saved the results of your computations, you would need an additional 1,104 days to process the new information.)

Method 2. You say to yourself, "I'll compute the fingerprints of all possible passwords, which will take time, and I'll store the resulting fingerprints in a big table. Then I'll have to find only a password fingerprint in the table to identify the corresponding password in the stolen data."

You will need $(9.54 \times 10^{16}) \times (12 + 32)$ bytes of memory because the task requires 12 bytes for the password and 32 bytes for the fingerprint if the fingerprint contains 256 bits (assuming an SHA256 function). That's 4.2×10^{18} bytes, or 4.2 million hard disks with a capacity of one terabyte.

This memory requirement is too large. Method 2 is no more feasible than method 1. Method 1 requires too many computations, and method 2 requires too much memory. Both cases are problematic: either each new password takes too long to compute, or precomputing all possibilities and storing all the results is too large a task.

Is there some compromise that requires less computing power than method 1 and less memory than required for method 2? Indeed, there is. In 1980 Martin Hellman of Stanford University suggested an approach that was improved in 2003 by Philippe Oechslin of the Swiss Federal Institute of Technology in Lausanne and further refined more recently by Gildas Avoine of the National Institute of Applied Sciences of Rennes (INSA Rennes) in France. It demands less computing power than method 1 in exchange for using a little more memory.

The Beauty of the Rainbow

Here is how it works: First, we need a function R that transforms a fingerprint $h(P)$ into a new password $R(h(P))$. One might, for instance, consider fingerprints as numbers written in the binary numeral system and consider passwords as numbers written in the K numeral system, where K is the number of allowable symbols for passwords. Then the function R converts data from the binary numeral system to the K numeral system. For every fingerprint $h(P)$, it computes a new password $R(h(P))$.

Now, with this function R, we can precompute data tables called rainbow tables (so named perhaps because of the multicolored way these tables are depicted).

To generate a data point in this table, we start from a possible password P_0, compute its fingerprint, $h(P_0)$ and then compute a new possible password $R(h(P_0))$, which becomes P_1. Next, we continue this process from P_1. Without storing anything other than P_0, we compute the sequence P_1, P_2,... until the fingerprint starts with 20 zeros; that fingerprint is designated $h(P_n)$. Such a fingerprint occurs only once in about 1,000,000 fingerprints because the result of a hash function is similar to result of a uniform random draw, and 220 is roughly equal to 1,000,000. The password/fingerprint pair [P0, $h(P_n)$], containing the fingerprint that starts with 20 zeros is then stored in the table.

A very large number of pairs of this type are computed. Each password/fingerprint pair [P_0, $h(P_n)$] represents the sequence of passwords P_0, P_1,... P_n and their fingerprints, but the table does not store those intermediate calculations. The table thus lists many password/fingerprint pairs and represents many more (the intermediates, such as P_1 and P_2, that can be derived from the listed pairs). But, of course, there may be gaps: some passwords may be absent from all the chains of calculations.

For a good database with almost no gaps, the memory needed to store the calculated pairs is a million times smaller than that needed for method 2, as described earlier. That is less than four one-terabyte hard disks. Easy. Also, as will be seen, using the table to derive passwords from stolen fingerprints is quite doable.

Let us see how the data stored on the hard disks makes it possible to determine a password in a given space in just a few seconds. Assume that there are no gaps; precomputation of the table takes into account all the passwords of a designated type—for example, 12-character passwords taken from the 26 letters of the alphabet.

A fingerprint f_0 in a stolen data set can be used to reveal the associated password in the following way. Calculate $h(R(f_0))$ to arrive at a new fingerprint, f_1, then calculate $h(R(f_1))$ to get f_2, and so on, until you get to a fingerprint that begins with 20 zeros: f_m. Then check the table to see which original password, P_0, the fingerprint f_m is associated with. Based on P_0, calculate the passwords and fingerprints h_1, h_2,.... that follow until you inevitably generate the original fingerprint f_0, designated hk. The password you are looking for is the one that gave rise to h_k—in other words, $R(h_k - 1)$, which is one step earlier in the chain of calculations.

The computation time required is what it takes to look for f_m in the table plus the time needed to compute the sequence of fingerprints from the associated password $(h_1, h_2,..., h_k)$—which is about a million times shorter than the time needed to compute the table itself. In other words, the time needed is quite reasonable.

Thus, doing a (very long) precomputation and storing only part of the results makes it possible to retrieve any password with a known fingerprint in a reasonable amount of time.

To summarize, by knowing the beginning and end of each chain of computations (the only things that are stored during precomputation), a hacker can retrieve any password from a fingerprint. In somewhat simplistic terms, starting from a stolen fingerprint—call it fingerprint X—a hacker would apply the R and h functions repeatedly, calculating a series of passwords and fingerprints until reaching a fingerprint with 20 zeros in front of it. The hacker would then look up that final fingerprint in the table (Fingerprint C in the example below) and identify its corresponding password (Password C).

Sample Table Excerpt

Password A—Fingerprint A

Password B—Fingerprint B

Password C—Fingerprint C

Password D—fingerprint D

Next, the hacker would apply the h and R functions again, beginning with the identified password, continuing on until one of the resulting fingerprints in the chain matches the stolen fingerprint:

Sample Calculation

Password C $\rightarrow$ fingerprint 1 $\rightarrow$ password 2- $\rightarrow$ fingerprint 2 $\rightarrow$ password 3.... $\rightarrow$ password 22- $\rightarrow$ fingerprint 23 [a match to fingerprint X!]

The match (fingerprint 23) would indicate that the previous password (password 22), from which the fingerprint was derived, is the one linked to the stolen fingerprint.

Many computations must be done to establish the first and last column of the rainbow table. By storing only the data in these two columns and by recomputing the chain, hackers can identify any password from its fingerprint.

About the Author

Jean-Paul Delahaye is a professor emeritus of computer science at the University of Lille in France and a researcher at the Research Center in Computer Science, Signal and Automatics of Lille (CRIStAL). He recently published Les Mathématiciens Se Plient au Jeu *(Belin, 2017), a French collection of articles from* Pour la Science.

How Cryptojacking Can Corrupt the Internet of Things

By Larry Greenemeier

C yber criminals shut down parts of the Web in October 2016 by attacking the computers that serve as the internet's switchboard. Their weapon of choice? Poorly secured Web cameras and other internet-connected gadgets that have collectively come to be known as the Internet of Things (IoT). The attack created a minor panic among people trying to visit Sony PlayStation Network, Twitter, GitHub and Spotify's Web sites, but it had little long-term effect on internet use or the hijacked devices. Less than two years later, however, security experts are sounding the alarm over a new and possibly more nefarious type of IoT attack that "cryptojacks" smart devices, surreptitiously stealing their computing power to help cyber criminals make digital money.

Cryptocurrencies—so called because they use cryptography to secure transactions and mint new virtual coins—are generated when computers loaded with "cryptomining" software perform complex mathematical calculations. The calculations themselves serve no practical purpose, but the faster the computers complete them the more electronic money they make. Cryptojacking (a mashup of the words "cryptocurrency" and "hijacking") occurs anytime someone uses another person's internet-connected device without permission to "mine" Ethereum, Monero or some other virtual cash. (Bitcoins are a lot more valuable, but this well-known cryptocurrency is more likely to be created using warehouses of servers rather than someone's stolen processing power).

Cyber criminals steal that power by sneaking malicious software containing cryptomining code onto PCs, smartphones and other internet-connected devices that, once infected, divert some of their processors' capacity into solving the aforementioned calculations. Another type of cryptojacking attack occurs when internet users are tricked into visiting Web sites containing code that grabs part of their device's processing power for as long as they visit the site. To entice people to stay, those sites tend to offer free pornography or pirated content. Victims usually have no idea their device has been coopted—although they might wonder why their batteries drain so quickly.

"When mining for gold, the person who works hardest with their pickaxe makes the most money," says Richard Enbody, an associate computer science and engineering professor at Michigan State University. "In cryptomining, the pickaxe is an algorithm. The more complex the calculations it performs, the more processing power and energy it uses and the more money it earns."

The latest trend is for criminals to infect appliances and other internet-connected devices with unwanted cryptomining software, Sherri Davidoff, CEO of cyber security firm LMG Security, said during a recent IoT cryptojacking webinar. "Many of these devices are unmonitored and highly vulnerable to simple attacks that exploit weak passwords and unpatched vulnerabilities," Davidoff said. Nearly every case LMG is currently investigating has turned up cryptomining software, in addition to whatever other malware criminals installed on their victims' computers, she added.

To test IoT devices' susceptibility to having their processors hijacked to make cryptocurrency, Davidoff and her colleagues hacked into a Web camera in their lab and installed cryptomining software. After a day of calculating the camera managed to produce about three-quarters of a penny's worth of Monero. Not exactly the motherlode, but those almost-pennies add up over time—especially if an attacker takes over thousands of Web cameras and leaves the software in place for a while, Davidoff said. Security cameras are a prime target because they connect to mostly unsecured public networks and are fairly generic—the same malware can be used to infect many different brands. In some cases these devices do not allow users to change their default security passwords.

"For financially-motivated cybercriminals, cryptojacking a large number of inadequately protected IoT devices could be highly lucrative," says Pranshu Bajpai, a PhD candidate in Michigan State University's Department of Computer Science and Engineering. "It can be argued that gaining [an] initial foothold into IoT devices is relatively easier than a computer or a phone, which normally have better protections." Given that many IoT devices lack updated antivirus software or an intrusion detection system, the malware is more likely to remain undetected longer.

In addition to degrading battery life, cryptojacking can strain or possibly burn out a device's processor. In an extreme case LMG investigated, one of the client's employees requested an extremely powerful computer—ostensibly for work—only to inform the client within a couple of months that the computer had caught fire. A few weeks later the client discovered that the employee had been using his new work computer for cryptomining. Most cryptominers and hackers avoid overtaxing their machines, or the machines they hijack, for fear of killing a (digital) cash cow. Still, even if cryptojacking does not destroy a device it will slow it down considerably.

Not all remote cryptomining is done on the sly or for malicious purposes. In February lifestyle magazine *Salon* employed the practice to help make up for the advertising revenue they lose when readers use ad-blocking software. *Salon* began asking online readers to help support the publication financially, either by shutting off ad blockers or allowing *Salon* to borrow users' devices for Monero mining while they read. UNICEF Australia encourages people to donate their computers' processing power to the charity for digital fundraising. Cryptojacking, however, is increasingly being recognized as a crime. A Japanese court earlier this month sentenced a man to a year in prison for illegally cryptomining $45 in Monero on victims' computers.

People can protect their devices primarily by keeping their operating systems and software up to date, Bajpai says. They can also install programs called "extensions," which block mining software, in their Web browsers. Consumers typically must rely on the companies that make internet routers, Web cameras and other connected devices to keep that technology secure and up to date.

If those companies do not ship their products with secure software and update it frequently to fight malware, the IoT could be in for a bumpy ride—and it is expected to grow from about 23 billion devices this year to more than 75 billion by 2025.

About the Author

Larry Greenemeier is the associate editor of technology for Scientific American, *covering a variety of tech-related topics, including biotech, computers, military tech, nanotech and robots.*

GLOSSARY

artificial intelligence Technology that allows a computer to imitate human thinking and decision-making.

blockchain A decentralized public ledger of transactions that no one person or company owns or controls.

data breach Unauthorized access to information stored on Internet-connected storage equipment.

encryption Conversion of human-readable information into a hidden code.

hacker A computer expert who tests computer security systems (a "white hat") or breaks into them (a "black hat").

infrastructure The system of public resources of a region, such as transportation, electrical grid, sewers and water.

malware Software written for malicious purposes.

phishing Attempt to trick someone into revealing personal data online.

quantum computing Computing that uses the properties of subatomic particles to perform calculations and functions.

ransomware Malware that requires a victim to pay a ransom in order to access their encrypted files.

vulnerability Capability of being attacked or damaged.

FURTHER INFORMATION

"What Is a Cyber Attack?," IBM, https://www.ibm.com/topics/cyber-attack.

Boehm, Jim, James Kaplan, and Wolf Richter. "Safeguarding Against Cyberattack in an Increasingly Digital World," McKinsey Digital, June 30, 2020, https://www.mckinsey.com/capabilities/mckinsey-digital/our-insights/safeguarding-against-cyberattack-in-an-increasingly-digital-world.

Bushwick, Sophie. "Ultrasonic Attack Device Hacks Phones through Solid Objects," *Scientific American,* March 18, 2020, https://www.scientificamerican.com/article/ultrasonic-attack-device-hacks-phones-through-solid-objects/.

Greenemeier, Larry. "Phone Hacking Fears and Facts," *Scientific American,* April 20, 2016, https://www.scientificamerican.com/article/phone-hacking-fears-and-facts/.

Mazzetti, Mark. "Biden Acts to Restrict U.S. Government Use of Spyware," *New York Times,* March 27, 2023, https://www.nytimes.com/2023/03/27/us/politics/biden-spyware-executive-order.html.

Sanger, David E. and Julian E. Barnes. "U.S. Hunts Chinese Malware That Could Disrupt American Military Operations," *New York Times,* July 29, 2023, https://www.nytimes.com/2023/07/29/us/politics/china-malware-us-military-bases-taiwan.html.

Wats, Valentine. "Why Technology, Not More Legislation, Is the Answer for Cybersecurity," *Forbes,* August 17, 2023, https://www.forbes.com/sites/forbestechcouncil/2023/08/17/why-technology-not-more-legislation-is-the-answer-for-cybersecurityvalentine-wats/?sh=7edf158c3252.

CITATIONS

1.1 AI-Influenced Weapons Need Better Regulation by Branka Marijan (March 30, 2022); 1.2 Are We Ready for the Future of Warfare? by Terry C. Wallace, Jr. (September 4, 2018); 1.3 Fully Autonomous Weapons Pose Unique Dangers to Humankind by Noel Sharkey (February 1, 2020); 1.4 Here's How to End the Fog of Cyber War by The Editors (June 1, 2016); 1.5 Here's What a Cyber Warfare Arsenal Might Look Like by Larry Greenemeier (May 6, 2015); 2.1 Hacker Attack on Essential Pipeline Shows Infrastructure Weaknesses by Sophie Bushwick (May 12, 2021); 2.2 How Hackers Tried to Add Dangerous Lye into a City's Water Supply by Sophie Bushwick (February 12, 2021); 2.3 Is the Power Grid Getting More Vulnerable to Cyber Attacks? by Jesse Dunietz (August 23, 2017); 2.4 The Most Vulnerable Ransomware Targets Are the Institutions We Rely On Most by Annie Sneed (March 23, 2016); 2.5 U.S. Hospitals Not Immune to Crippling Cyber Attacks by Dina Fine Maron (May 15, 2017); 2.6 Urban Bungle: Atlanta Cyber Attack Puts Other Cities on Notice by Larry Greenemeier (April 4, 2018); 2.7 What Do Hurricanes and Cybersecurity Have in Common? by Algirde Pipikaite, Haiyan Song (October 29, 2019); 3.1 Blockchain Enhances Privacy, Security and Conveyance of Data by Mihaela Ulieru (June 23, 2016); 3.2 Data Thieves Find Easy Pickings in the Health Care System by Adam Tanner (July 27, 2016); 3.3 Data Vu: Why Breaches Involve the Same Stories Again and Again by Daniel J. Solove, Woodrow Hartzog (July 26, 2022); 3.4 Giant U.S. Computer Security Breach Exploited Very Common Software by Sophie Bushwick (December 15, 2020); 3.5 The Equifax Hack–Bad for Them, Worse for Us by Paul Rosenzweig (September 12, 2017); 4.1 Are Blockchains the Answer for Secure Elections? Probably Not by Jesse Dunietz (August 16, 2018); 4.2 How to Defraud Democracy by J. Alex Halderman, Jen Schwartz (September 1, 2019); 4.3 The Vulnerabilities of Our Voting Machines by Jen Schwartz (November 1, 2018); 5.1 CSI: Cyber-Attack Scene Investigation–a Malware Whodunit by Larry Greenemeier (January 28, 2016); 5.2 FBI Takes Down Hive Criminal Ransomware Group by Sophie Bushwick (January 31, 2023); 5.3 Hacking the Ransomware Problem by The Editors (January 1, 2022); 5.4 The Imperfect Crime: How the WannaCry Hackers Could Get Nabbed by Jesse Dunietz (August 16, 2017); 5.5 Women in Cybersecurity: Where We Are and Where We're Going by Nahal Shahidzadeh (September 23, 2019); 6.1 Congressional Ignorance Leaves the U.S. Vulnerable to Cyberthreats by Jackson Barnett (October 21, 2019); 6.2 Misdiagnosing Our Cyberhealth by Emily Balcetis (August 4, 2020); 6.3 Passwords Are on the Way Out, and It's about Time by David Pogue (August 1, 2016); 6.4 Social Security Numbers Aren't Secure: What Should We Use Instead? by Sophie Bushwick (September 24, 2021); 6.5 The Mathematics of (Hacking) Passwords by Jean-Paul Delahaye (April 12, 2019); 6.6 How Cryptojacking Can Corrupt the Internet of Things by Larry Greenemeier (July 31, 2018).

Each author biography was accurate at the time the article was originally published.

Content originally published on or after July 1, 2018, was reproduced with permission. Copyright 2024 Scientific American, a Division of Springer Nature America, Inc. All rights reserved.

Content originally published from January 1, 2010, to June 30, 2018, was reproduced with permission. Copyright 2024 Scientific American, a Division of Nature America, Inc. All rights reserved.

INDEX

A

Argentina, 79–80
artificial intelligence, 8–11,
    14–16, 19–20

B

Balcetis, Emily, 126–129
Barnett, Jackson, 123–125
blockchain, 60–62, 79–83,
    114–116
Britain, 13, 48–49, 63, 102
Buchanan, Ben, 36–38, 71–74
Bushwick, Sophie, 32–38,
    71–74, 105–109, 133–136

C

China, 10, 13–14, 16, 19,
    25–27, 29, 42, 85, 96, 127
COVID-19, 37
cryptocurrency, 44, 51–52,
    60–61, 79–82, 108, 113–
    116, 152–155
cryptojacking, 152–155
cybersecurity, 43, 47, 55–58,
    67–74, 76, 79, 82, 84, 95,
    102–104, 111, 117–121,
    123–125, 134, 138

D

data breach/theft, 25, 63–65,
    67–77, 101–102, 108, 127,
    134–135, 137

data collection/minimization,
    67–70
Delahaye, Jean-Paul, 137–151
drone, 9, 15–16, 18–19
Dunietz, Jesse, 39–43, 79–83,
    113–116

E

election, 79–98, 123–125
encryption, 13–14, 44, 51–53,
    69, 105–107, 110, 138,
    140, 145

G

Germany, 13, 18
GPS, 12–13, 20, 22–23, 29
Greenemeier, Larry, 27–30,
    51–54, 101–104, 152–155

H

Halderman, J. Alex, 84–99
Hartzog, Woodrow, 67–70

I

India, 9, 131
infrastructure targets, 8–9, 12,
    26, 29
    electric grid, 9, 12, 28, 33,
        39–43, 46, 101
    financial, 12, 25, 28, 33, 56,
        76

government, 25, 33, 44–45, 51–55, 71–74, 101, 110

health care, 12–13, 33, 44–46, 48–50, 52, 76, 107, 110–111, 113

oil/gas, 15, 32–35, 41, 56

telecommunications, 12, 22, 28, 52, 113

transportation, 12, 22, 33, 52, 55, 113

water, 36–38, 46, 51

Iran, 25, 28, 37, 42–43, 85

Israel, 9, 18, 23, 25, 28

L

Lee, Robert M., 39–43

M

malware, 9, 13, 28, 32–35, 44–55, 69, 93, 96–97, 101–116, 152–155

Marijan, Branka, 8–11

Maron, Dina Fine, 48–50

N

North Korea, 27, 29, 42, 85, 96, 104

P

password, 130–132, 134, 137–151

phishing, 67, 111, 128

Pipikaite, Algirde, 55–58

Pogue, David, 130–132

privacy, 60–62, 123–155

R

Rosenzweig, Paul, 75–77

Russia, 8–10, 16–19, 21–23, 25–27, 37, 39, 42, 55, 73, 84–88, 94–98, 101, 108, 123

S

Schwartz, Jen, 84–99

Shahidzadeh, Nahal, 117–121

Sharkey, Noel, 15–24

Sneed, Annie, 44–47

social media, 10, 14, 94, 126

social security number, 133–136

Solove, Daniel J., 67–70

Song, Haiyan, 55–58

South Korea, 29, 42

Syria, 15, 18

T

Tanner, Adam, 63–66

U

Ukraine, 8, 10, 12, 40, 42–43, 101, 108

Ulieru, Mihaela, 60–62

United Nations, 8, 11, 17, 23, 26

W

Wallace, Terry C., Jr., 12–14

war, 8–30, 42

weapons, 8–11, 15–25, 28–29

Wolff, Josephine, 32–35, 105–109